The city of Talfryn, where Elazar will celebrate the end of the millennium at the *"Wizards of the Kingdoms"* festival.

Discover the Alchemy of Life and Death!

"There are six words that represent the alchemy of life and death. They must be said consecutively, and when all the lights have lit up along the sides of this crystal flower in the center, the goddess will leave the higher realms, and return to us."

On one side of the crystal was the inscription, *"Alchemy of Life,"* while on the other side was written, *"Alchemy of Death."*

"I hope you know what the code words are, because I have no idea," said Galax.

"Yes, I do," said Silvica. "Stand back, while I activate the crystal."

Galax and Justise stepped sideways a few feet, and watched Silvica take a long, meditative breath. For several minutes she looked directly at the first orb disk in the wall.

The Keys of Fate

TOWER OF CHANGE

Written and Illustrated
By Tina M. Randolph

Rhapsody Publishing

Rhapsody Publishing
PO Box 727
Fresno, Texas 77545

THE KEYS OF FATE: TOWER OF CHANGE

AGES 9 AND UP

www.rhapsodypublishing.com

ISBN-10: 0-9841024-0-X
ISBN-13: 978-0984102402

Visit the Author at
www.tinamrandolph.com

Cover Design
by Tina M. Randolph

Printed in the U.S.A.

First Edition/December 2010

"We are all one body, and key players in the game called life." –Tina M. Randolph

For My Mother,
Jimmie Mae Butler,
Who Has Transcended This World
You Were My Greatest Encourager,
And You Are Greatly Missed

For Millicent Anne Butler
My Dear Sister,
Who Gave Me Inspiration

And For Jyoti Amge,
The Littlest Girl In The World,
Who Dreams Of Being A Bollywood Star
I Have Written A Part
Especially For You,
May All Your Wishes Come True

CONTENTS

Solve the Riddle

"The key to the truth is locked away,
like a mystery in a prism.
The answer eludes you.

When Twilight comes,
the Dawn follows."

- Sidonias Elazar -

The Keys of Fate

TOWER OF CHANGE

Chapter One
Tower of Change

GALAX Hanz smiled with enthusiasm as Sidonias Elazar announced he would soon be leaving for his time-honored trip to Talfryn. He—being the wizard's apprentice—would be responsible for the castle while Elazar was away. It was perhaps the greatest honor he could have ever been given. In Talfryn, Sidonias would be meeting with a few of his fellow allies—other wizards like him—to celebrate the end of the millennium, before the new one began.

Sidonias was an oddly reclusive fellow, and rarely left his home for any reason. He was always on guard, and kept strict watch over the tower—that no one—not even Galax was allowed to enter. He had protected it for almost a thousand years, and Galax

expected that any day now, Sidonias would be opening the doors for the millennial ritual. He wasn't sure
what that ceremony entailed, but he knew it was
monumental and historic at least.

The old wizard was satisfied with the progress
his young apprentice was making, and therefore, he
decided Galax was ready to use the secret enchantments that in the last twelve years, he had taught
him to master.

Galax, however, feared he was not prepared to
protect the treasures that were hidden within the
walls of the tower. He saw himself as needing a lot
more experience and proficiency at his craft. Even
though he felt somewhat inadequate about being the
guardian of the tower, he accepted his duty, and was
slowly beginning to find the whole idea fascinating.

There were plenty of antiquities in Elazar's study
that Galax had not even attempted to examine, and
so he figured he would do some exploring, as soon as
the ancient one was out of the way.

Galax was twenty-two, and attractive, though
he wasn't very social, and hardly spent any time with
others his own age. He was the average height, with
an athletic build and deep penetrating eyes.

Days began to seem like months to Galax, as he
waited patiently for Sidonias to take his leave. He was
growing anxious by the minute for privacy, spending
all his time gazing into various sized orbs and read-

ing every book he could find on unlocking doors and chests that were cast with spells.

A strange visitor appeared in the *Emerald of Trillia* one evening, wearing a wizard's cloak, and carrying a golden scepter. He rode towards the castle on a beautiful white horse. The wizard appeared to be taking his precious time, stopping occasionlly to write down notes on a long piece of parchment, and whistling to himself a song of the faeries. He tarried for a while in the apple orchards of Crickslade, before mounting his stallion and continuing on his crossing to Fanya. Galax reported the sighting to Sidonias right away, and was immediately sent out to greet the old friend, carrying a satchel of food and a flask of fresh water.

The wizard was named Mortighan, and he would be leaving with Sidonias for the celebration in Talfryn. Galax met Mortighan between the lakes of Jaziel, and the forest of Fanya, which was only twenty miles from the castle mount. He was sitting on a large rock, chewing on a fig, throwing stones into the rippling lake, when the weary wizard dismounted his horse and strode up to greet him.

"Good day. You must be Galax. How is my old friend, Elazar?" Mortighan asked.

"Quite well, *sir*. And he is looking forward to seeing you," responded Galax, handing over the flask.

"Oh, you can call me Morti."

3

"Very well, then *Morti*," Galax replied.

As Mortighan drank the cold water, he smiled merrily, envisioning Elazar telling his old stories again. He was anxious to discuss the details of the new millennium with him.

"I know I shouldn't be asking you this, but have you ever been in the castle tower? Sidonias has never let me inside," Galax questioned. He wasn't sure Mortighan would reveal anything useful that he could use to break the spell.

Galax had made up his mind days before that he would find a way to temporarily reverse the spell of protection, so he could uncover the truth of the

tower. There would only be a short time to get in, get out, and put everything back in place before his master returned. Now he wasn't sure if he should even consider the risky attempt at all.

To his surprise, Mortighan readily answered, "Actually, I have been in the *'Tower of Change'* once before. It was a very long time ago. So long, that I was probably about your age when it happened. Back then the tower was guarded by a powerful wizard named Delphi. He was from another dimension, and he brought to our world of Amunet, the magic of his kind."

Galax listened earnestly to every word that Mortighan said, and invited him to sit down and have a portion of his lunch, which was a lump of bread, and a morsel of cheese and meat. Mortighan dipped his scrap of wheat bread into the cheese spread, took a big bite, chewed for a moment, and then continued his account.

"Delphi entrusted Elazar with the most precious duty, *there was*. He chose him to guard the *fate of the world*."

"*Really*—what do you mean—guard the *fate of the world*?" Galax repeated.

"Yes, *fate*," answered Mortighan. "He was literally holding the *key* to it."

Mortighan considered for a moment if he should tell any more of the story to Galax. It was not his responsibility to enlighten him on the subject of Delphi, but instead he decided to continue on with his telling.

"Delphi translated over a thousand years ago. He moved over into another sphere during the battle against the King's Mage, Leodon. He did everything he could to protect the tower. In the end, he had no choice but to take Leodon with him to another dimension," said Mortighan.

"I can't believe all of this has been kept from me," Galax blustered. "Why?"

"To protect you and the world you live in, *my boy*. Now, I can tell you no more," he gestured, waving Galax aside, frowning at the images that seemed to be popping up in his head. "I have probably told you enough already. You'll have to ask Elazar if you want to know more," he insisted, mounting his stallion and drawing up his reins to depart from the area.

His master's disapproving eyes resonated through his mind. Galax cued his stallion, *Sugar Cane*, signaling him to catch up with Mortighan, who was already disappearing over the horizon.

Galax was glad Mortighan had finally arrived. This meant that he and Sidonias would be leaving soon for Talfryn. He wasn't sure exactly how many days before their departure, but then that wasn't important. All he had to do was prepare for when the time came.

Mortighan and Sidonias greeted each other with warm hugs. "I missed you Morti, old friend," Elazar exclaimed, smiling so happily that Galax was moved by his sincerity.

"And *you*...you haven't changed a bit," chuckled Mortighan, patting him happily on the back.

"I'll put your scepter away, Morti," Galax said, after the guest had laid down his belongings. He watched the two of them head for the balcony on the second floor, so they could catch up on old times.

Galax took the shiny golden scepter into the room of relics. There were many rooms in the castle. One with precious stones that had incredible powers, and others like the room of *orbs*, the *library of spell books*, the room of *chemicals, elixirs, and fumes*, the closet-sized room of *ancient contraptions*, and the largest of rooms held *antiquities, oddities, and relics*—all contained in various-sized chests.

Sneezing as he opened a dusty, dragon-head chest, he dropped the scepter into its compartment, and closed the top sharply. There was no need to lock it, because the entrance to the room of relics was well hidden, and wasn't visible to the naked eye.

In order to see it, you would have to say a special chant, while standing in a particular spot in the hallway.

Galax had repeated the chant three times before the door appeared, and it was even harder to find your way out, once you had entered.

"The boy doesn't know what he's up against, Elazar," Mortighan said, as he lit a pipe and began to smoke.

"What makes you think that?" questioned Elazar. "That boy is gifted, and ready for even the most challenging of tasks. He may not know how serious his charge is, but he is definitely well taught, and ready for anything."

"Well, if you say so, but he asked me about the tower, and I was surprised you hadn't told him."

"Yes, I was planning on telling him as little as possible. I think it's best that the contents of that tower be not known to anyone, unless it's absolutely necessary. Don't you agree?" asked Elazar, gazing over the balcony at the forest of Fanya, watching the sun descend slowly from view.

Mortighan nodded approvingly, releasing a puff of smoke that filled the air with a leafy fragrance. "You and I are the only ones who truly understand the celebration in Talfryn. Our discussion about the new millennium has much greater value than presumed by the council. The advisement received there will help me in the ritual, and the time is almost at hand," said Elazar, taking out a small glass tube, and drinking a glowing aquamarine liquid from it. White trails of sparkling mists swirled around his mouth as he coughed.

"You are right. I just hope the damage isn't too complicated to repair," Mortighan chuckled. "It's hard enough as it is to *undo* what has already been done."

"Let us retire for a while. I'll bet you are tired from your travels, my friend," said Elazar.

"Yes, of course. I presume that we'll be leaving in the morning?"

"...at the crack of dawn. Will that be enough time for you to rest up?" asked Elazar.

He pointed his hand towards the door, showing Mortighan where he would be retiring for the night.

"I shall be refreshed and ready to leave," Mortighan said as he passed him.

They had stepped directly into a large guest room lit by fire-light. It gave off warmth that felt very welcoming to Mortighan's shivering skin. He went directly over to the fireplace, placed his cold hands over the flames, and tossed his long white beard over his shoulders, so his face could soak up the heat.

Smiling, Elazar waved goodnight to Mortighan, and closed the door behind him. In Fanya, and especially on castle mount, the temperature dropped drastically after sunset, turning chillingly cold, but only until the early hours of the morning, before the sun showed its glowing face again.

Elazar found Galax reading in his study. He was staring quite inquisitively at an old book of spells called *Perfect World Magic*, which had been taken off the shelf a few days before for dusting, but was never put back again.

"Galax, my young apprentice, I am glad to see you so engrossed in your studies."

"Yes, Elazar, I am very interested in the old ways," he said. "This book dates back more than seven thousand years. I can hardly decipher the language it is written in."

"Morti has expressed to me that you inquired about the tower," Elazar said, in a fatherly voice. "Is there anything you wish to speak with me about?"

Galax felt a tad embarrassed by this remark, and tried to hide his face farther into the book he was now pretending to read. His eyes were widening considerably, and he felt his hair stand completely on end.

Elazar did not press the point. He waited for a moment to see if Galax would respond to his questioning.

He hesitated.

"I know you are still wondering about the *Tower of Change*, but...it is for your own good that you know as little as possible."

Galax was quiet. He continued to peer into the heavy book, keeping his eyes averted towards its bottom pages. He was still feeling uncomfortable about the topic they were discussing, knowing that he should have asked Elazar directly for answers, instead of going to his oldest friend.

For years, Elazar had always instructed Galax to stay clear of the tower, and never to ask him anything about it. He had warned him many times that he was not permitted to *even think* about what kind of magic lay hidden there, and he was to guard its secrets from the rest of the world, with his life.

"Galax, you have been chosen by me to watch over the tower. It is a great responsibility. So don't let me down," Elazar said.

"I won't, Master. I will guard the tower with my life. You can count on me!" Galax blurted out confidently.

"Good," said Elazar. "We'll be leaving tomorrow."

After a few moments, Galax lifted his head up from the book, and watched Elazar leave the room. I should ask him, he told himself. *I should just ask him, now.* However, something deep inside of him kept him pinned to his seat. He wanted to know exactly what magic lay hidden in the tower, and what could possibly be so important that it had to be kept secret, even from him. He glanced towards the door that Elazar exited, as if he was expecting him to return at any moment and tell him more details. Even if he didn't, Galax knew he hadn't yet found an answer to solving the riddles for entering the chamber, but all he had to do was keep searching through the texts.

He was reading speedily now, glancing at each page with determination. He would be left in privacy by morning, and he knew he had to be ready to break the charms surrounding the tower's entrance.

He looked up, but Elazar hadn't returned. It was getting late now, and the lamp that he'd lit, which was sitting near him on the wooden desk, was beginning to dim. Galax was losing hope. The main spell he was looking for was a mystery to him. He wasn't even sure of what it was he was supposed to be reading. He just decided he would pretend he was Elazar, and guess at what magic he might have used. It was like searching for a ladybug in a cornfield.

After an hour, Galax closed the book that he'd been reading, and sat still for a moment, contemplating his next move. *I wonder where I should look? What would Elazar do if he were me? Where would he be hiding a spell?*

He relaxed his frown. Leaning comfortably back in his chair, he folded his arms around the back of his head. His mind was drifting now. He imagined the sweet smell of summer's fragrance, and wondered how long it would be before he could go into the city of Talfryn again. He could see the busy streets of the marketplace, crawling with young apprentices, haggling to buy whatever new relics the caravan from Gregale had brought in. There was always something intriguing to purchase and bring back to Elazar.

The last time he was there, which was in the spring season, he had unexpectedly stumbled upon a very rare item, called a *Liimer Star*, which was a star-shaped gemstone that had fallen from the neighboring moon of Duldron.

The stone was a misty white color, and had special powers of universal knowledge. Because it had traveled through space, shooting into Amunet's atmosphere, it was said to contain the images of the time continuum it had traveled in. It only held the knowledge in coordinates on the vertices of the star, which it had tracked through the orbiting planet before it touched down.

When he had first presented the remnant to Elazar, he was very delighted. He said it had taken over a thousand years to travel the distance from Duldron to Amunet. He was fascinated with the many uses that the *Liimer Star* could offer him, especially in his visions and reminiscences. Galax had seen him use the star once to show him the past, but there was a specific way in which the star had to be accessed in order to gain the insight the seeker was seeking.

There was a definite trick to turning the star and producing a halo shield. The shield was like a see-through window, and once the star produced this portal—a person could visit the past, as if they were standing in the place where the event happened.

The visual was three dimensional, yet you could only view it from the location of the halo.

Galax had not learned to spin the star, and had only watched Elazar do it once before. There were no instruction manuals that he knew of, and nothing in the ancient texts that suggested it could be performed without expertise, so he was quite perplexed about what his options were.

He sat up swiftly in his chair, and stretched. Again he had hit another road block. He was sure he could use the *Liimer Star*, but wondered how he would master the method. *I really have to think this through*, he said to himself.

He smiled brightly until his mouth had turned into an impish grin. He was up in a matter of seconds, heading towards the room of relics to locate the chest that held the *Liimer Star*. Once inside, he went from one chest to another, but could not remember where it had been kept.

Then he remembered. It wasn't in a chest at all, but hidden inside the starry painting that hung on the left wall. The only way to retrieve it was to reach into the shadows of the painting, and pull it out of the darkness of space.

"How hard could it be," he said aloud, placing the *Liimer Star* on the center round table. "Maybe I should just try it, and see if it works?"

He spun the star rapidly, and the room began

to warble and shake. The star was glowing vibrantly now, and making loud noises that he was sure would wake up Elazar.

"Or maybe *not*," he said smartly, putting it in his robe and quickly heading up the sandstone steps that led to his bed chamber.

Passing by Elazar's room, he placed his ear to the door and listened for any sounds that would tell him if he had awakened. After hearing Elazar's rhythmic breathing, he tipped-toed towards his own room, and sat the *Liimer Star* down on the bed. He had decided to wait until Elazar and Mortighan, had left the castle. This way, he could concentrate without fear of being discovered.

Galax lay on the bed holding the *Liimer Star* in front of him. He could not sleep, nor could he relax his mind. He was growing more anxious and restless by the minute. He found that if he turned the *Liimer Star* over in his hands, and rubbed its surface, he felt calmer.

By ancient tradition, it was Galax's option to receive a protection spell from his master when he was about to leave on a lengthy journey. This particular morning, he specifically requested one.

"You may have a special incantation that I have just recently written," Elazar suggested. "This one is strong enough to keep you protected from the most evil and darkest of spells."

"It is a good idea you asked for it. You can never be too careful with your duties. You know what needs to be *done*—" Mortighan added, staring Galax in his hazel eyes. "*You* are on a journey yourself...*I believe*?"

Galax replied insecurely, "Yes, Morti...I'm still learning the ways of my master. I have yet to reach his status of cleverness."

Mortighan and Elazar both chuckled at those words, turning to look at each other knowingly.

"You would be surprised, Galax," Mortighan said. "Elazar was quite foolish at your age."

"Yes, you *would* be surprised," Elazar repeated jovially." Now let us prepare for our trip, and get going."

After Elazar had cast the spell of protection on Galax, he and Mortighan mounted their stallions, and headed out towards Talfryn. It was only an hour before dawn, and just the right time for Galax to try out the *Liimer Star*.

Before he brought it down from his chamber, he placed a special cloth on the dining table, and watched Elazar's departure in a citrine orb. In the center of the gemstone, he saw that he and Mortighan had reached the forest of Fanya, and was headed to the East, towards the city of Winberlyn. Sure that he was long gone, and would not be returning soon, Galax raced to his bedroom and carefully picked up the *Liimer Star*.

The star was lighter than it was the day before, and he carried it in-between his robe and his shirt, protecting it from possibly slipping from his fingers and falling to the floor. If it accidentally shattered, he knew it would be nearly impossible to find another one on Amunet again. They were just that rare.

He wasn't sure where he wanted to practice his spinning, but he had two places in mind. The room of relics was one, where he was the night before, and the room of orbs was another, which he thought he would rather be, in case he needed to use the orb again.

The room of orbs was a round room, on the first floor of the northern tower. Although the room wasn't that large, it was big enough for him to have plenty of space, and wide enough for even a few hundred more orbs to be brought in from Talfryn.

The room was well lit by tiny diamond-shaped windows that covered every inch of the walls. The sunlight shown in brightly from the portholes, while an even more vibrant illumination glowed from a variety of twenty-two orbs, as some of them were instantly activated when Galax stepped into the room.

This was the first time he had ever been alone in the castle. Elazar had always been at home; he never gave him a chance to fully explore the specialty objects that he was sure would have caused suspicion if he had tried to investigate.

Now, there was nothing stopping him from using anything he needed to sneak into the *Tower of Change*. He was free to do as he pleased. Elazar would not be coming back for at least a fortnight, and that would give him plenty of time to find out what was kept in dire secret.

Chapter Two
The Armored-Fish Egg

WITH sweat dripping down his face, Galax set the *Liimer Star* on the glass table in the center of the room. *I've got to remember how Elazar did it. Did he place it on the table, or was it doing something else?*

He was trying desperately to remember. He knew that when Elazar had spun it, neither the room shook nor the walls warbled. If he handled the artifact incorrectly, the whole castle could tremble so forcibly, that any of the precious artifacts could get broken. Every item in the castle was unique and priceless to him. He was sure that it wouldn't do him any good to try spinning it the same way he had done the night before.

Holding out his hand, he rotated it in a half circle motion, causing the *Liimer Star* to lift slowly off the tabletop. When it was stationed about two feet above, he twirled his finger, this time gesturing it to spin counter-clockwise very rapidly. Suddenly, the *Liimer Star* began to flicker, creating a sheet of clear film that seemed to spread outward like a large disc. The star shone vibrantly from the center, and vanished into the disc, shooting speedily into what looked like space.

Focusing his attention on the now moving *Liimer Star*, he began searching the portal for the roof of the castle. "I know it passed over us," he said aloud.

Now all he had to do was to find the right moment in time when Elazar had cast the spell on the tower. He kept searching the image, but all he could see was the tops of trees, and a nearby lake. The large moon of Duldron was resting in the backdrop, and the night had turned from day to darkness, and back to daytime again.

The images were alternating so quickly, that Galax found it difficult to understand what he was seeing. After a long moment of watching flashes of colorful imagery, he threw up his hands in anguish.

The moment he lifted his hands, the images in the disc stopped motion, and rested on a small house on the edge of town. "Oh, so that's it," Galax said, enthusiastically. "I need to direct the vertices."

A few hand movements had brought him over the town of Gregale, and into the forest of Fanya. He was now looking directly at the castle, and wondering when in time it was. "How does it know what I am looking for?" he questioned.

Several swift movements, and he was inside the castle, watching Elazar in his early twenties, sitting at the same old desk, writing on a piece of parchment. "Great, so now all I have to do is figure out how to get him to open the door of the tower," Galax said.

"I *command* you to go and *open* the tower!" Galax shouted.

Nevertheless, nothing in the image changed. Elazar was still sitting in his chair, writing on his parchment, as tediously as he was before.

Galax wondered what to do. He was now facing a real challenge. He wasn't sure exactly what method he was supposed to be using. Elazar hadn't moved from his spot, and waving his hand only seemed to bring him to different locations in the portal.

Standing there bewildered, Galax thought for a long moment. *I wonder where the Liimer Star went. Maybe it is a steering device.* He reached into the portal, and moved his hand around inside. Once he felt the vertices of the *Liimer Star*, he pulled it out of the portal and turned it over a couple of times.

Immediately, Elazar faded into a blur, as time seemed to speed up. Now he was watching Elazar practicing his spells, and a few moments later he saw him riding a spotted horse in the woods.

Galax turned the star continuously until he found Elazar facing the large metal doors of the tower. He had stopped turning now, and was attentively observing the scene. Elazar put his hand beneath his robes near his chest, and pulled out a liquid vial hung around a black necklace. He had seen this necklace before, and was sure it contained an aquamarine liquid that he had always assumed was coughing medicine.

Elazar opened the glass vial, and drank two drops of the mystical liquid. A few moments later, he was seeing a faint figure of him separating from the first. The second figure, a ghostly form, put his hand directly through a glyph on the metal door and pulled out a semi-transparent, yet brightly lit key. Placing the key in the hand of his other self, he stepped easily back into his physical body again.

"Wow! That was *strange*!" exclaimed Galax. He wondered what wonderous liquid he was drinking, and why had he not used the key to open the door of the tower. Still he kept his eyes focused on Elazar, waiting to see what he would do next.

Elazar started speaking in an unknown language that he figured was perhaps a foreign one. During his incantation, glowing cryptic words appeared on a large translucent screen in mid-air. Then it vanished.

"What just happened?" Galax asked. "Am I *missing* something?"

He rotated the star carefully, rewinding the scene and watching it several more times. He was sure he was unable to read the message written on the screen. It was radiating a blue transparent color, and faded into the shape of a helix. Taking the key from his pocket, Elazar placed it into the center of the helix, and turned it once. Instantly, the first bolt on the door opened. However, there were two more locks underneath, which still hadn't unclasped.

Surprisingly, Elazar had disappeared, and returned a few seconds later. It happened so fast, that not even the turning of the *Liimer Star* was useful in figuring out where he had gone. Instantly, the second lock on the door unlatched, leaving only one lock left.

The unlocking of the third lock was the hardest to decipher. He saw Elazar place his hands on the door, and begin folding it into a small cube. Once he had done this, he fitted one of the keys into a hole in the cube, and turned it around. Not too soon afterwards, he and the cube were gone.

"Well," Galax said finally. "I don't know what just happened, but I *doubt* if I can duplicate it. I guess I don't have a choice though, if I want to see what's behind that door."

Placing the *Liimer Star* back inside the shield,

he watched the images fade out and the Liimer Star spinning vibrantly in midair. The light from the rotating star was so brilliant that Galax had to cover his eyes while he signaled the star to stop its spinning. Picking the star out of the air, he headed back to the room of relics to return it to its perpetual resting spot, back in the painting.

Now Galax hurried down the long corridor headed towards the room of *chemicals, elixirs, and fumes*, where he hoped to find a liquid like the one in the vial around Elazar's neck. There was a sudden aroma of fragrances and natural herbs filling his nostrils as he entered.

Galax was puzzled. He simply did not know what he was looking for. There were over fifteen hundred herbs, spices and elixirs bottled up and organized by alphabet. Some were categorized specifically by color, as well as a whole wall dedicated to essential oils and healing medicines.

He turned towards one of the aromatherapy oils and healing medicine shelves, lowering himself over a row of *magic* blends marked with symbols. One was indexed under astral travel, and branded with an ancient pictogram of a helix. This was not an aquamarine solution, and did not seem to have been recently used. The large glass jar was dusty, and the cap had several cobwebs on it.

"Perhaps I need to go and look in the chemistry

books in the study?" Galax murmured, perplexed. "I'm sure there must be a word or two about traveling outside of the body."

He was right. There were several books on astral travel, but nothing on how to mix an elixir for the experience. On the desk drawer in the study, was an ancient equation that Galax had to solve before he could open a hidden slot. It took several long hours, but he soon figured out the answer to be *infinity*.

The compartment contained several old scrolls, in which were written instructions for eleven herbs to enhance dreaming and inter-dimensional travel. One of the herbs was unique and known only as a myth to many wizards and apprentices.

This herb was a flower called *Aliya*, and was said to give back a lost life. *Aliya* was not known to exist in any place on Amunet. He especially had not encountered anyone who had ever seen this flower or used it in their magic potions. He wondered how Elazar would have managed to find the blossom, and utilize it to make his special mixture.

Two charts showed the combining of an aquamarine mixture, and next to it was a glyph that Galax had never seen before. One was a drawing of a man sitting with his legs crossed inside a pyramid, encircled inside a sphere, and the man, the pyramid, and the sphere were centered inside a cube. The text read: *The orb, which creates the illusion of ambience,*

*can be transformed into a reality that is paradise to
the Light Maker.*

Galax thought for a moment. "No, I doubt he
would go to the trouble of locating that flower. It
has to be something else, and hidden somewhere I'd
never think it would be." Glancing about the study,
he paused and said, "But *where*?"

Galax sat at the desk for a long while in deep con-
templation. It took him several minutes to recognize
what he was seeing. He was staring across the room,
gazing at a small stone pyramid, which was sitting
next to an elegant golden chalice, ornamented with
jewels. The chalice had been used by many wizards
before Elazar, to drink from the fountains of La Ewa,
which was said to have the power to render a person
invisible for several hours.

He was inspecting it purposefully, but it wasn't
the chalice that was catching his attention. It was a
large glass fishbowl. Swimming rapidly around in
the tank was an unusual species of aquatic life. He
thought he had seen a glimmering aquamarine bub-
ble coming from the fish's mouth, when suddenly he
remembered the reason his master was studying the
rare creature. Galax smiled, walked across the room
towards the specimen, and pulled out the papers and
record books Elazar had written on the non-tetrapod
chordate.

What he already knew about the fish was very

little, because he hadn't devoted much time to the studying of it. However, he was sure there was something unusual about the organism that kept Elazar constantly engrossed in investigating and researching a whole school of them, that he had hidden in the grotto on the grounds of the castle.

After carrying a skull over to the desk, he set a thick, leathery book down, opening it excitedly, flipping the pages in search of an explanation. He had an idea that the aquamarine bubbles were a clue to finding the elixir that Elazar had used for astral projection.

Galax had never noticed before, that from the bubbles, a luminous bright light emanated. The fish

was fat and dark, with thick armored scales, and globular onyx eyes that seemed to be watching his every move. It looked like a dangerously carnivorous creature, that would bite off his hand, if he was to breach its territory.

The records indicated that the fish laid magical eggs. The moment he saw the drawings of the gooey, clear, jelly-like yolk, and the aquamarine light coming from the center—he immediately knew he had stumbled across the answer. According to the text, these fish were called *Labrygillus* armored vertebrates that were extinct. This class of prehistoric organisms were bottom-dwellers, and predators.

Turning to face the golden chalice, he began planning his retrieval of a magic egg. He opened a cabinet, searching for the *water of La Ewa*, pulled out a crystal bottle, and poured the contents into the chalice.

The water felt smooth and flowed down his throat evenly. After a brief choking, his face began to disappear. The living liquid was making him transparent, and causing him quite a belly-ache. He looked at his hands and feet, and watched them slowly mystify into a sheer layer of glossy nothingness.

At the edge of the pond, in the darkness of the dimly lit grotto, Galax took off his heavy robes, and dived into the warm water. He went immediately down towards the bottom, and searched around for the location of the eggs. He checked the area as carefully as possible, not wanting to be unexpectedly attacked by any of the *Labrygillus*, and then swam further into the mysterious pool.

In the distance, he noticed a number of bright lights were glowing brilliant azure, nestled in a small area. Before he could even move towards the nest, he felt a huge *Labrygillus* swim up beside him and open its massive mouth. Galax didn't have a moment to spare. Even though he was invisible, the fish had somehow detected him, and was preparing an assault.

Galax's stomach started to gurgle, and he felt ill. The eggs were a few feet away, and he was getting dizzy from the lack of oxygen. Two enormous, wide mouthed, sharp-toothed, angry *Labrygillus* were heading straight towards him, one on each side of his body. He looked up, and broke into a desperate dog-paddle to the surface. Gasping for air, he ducked back underwater as quickly as he could, in order to see what the *Labrygillus* were doing.

To his amazement, both fish had disappeared, and so he made his way over to the drifting nest, and after grabbing a hefty egg, he emerged briefly to breathe. After a while, he reached the edge of the grotto, and climbed out safely. He was dripping water footprints as he put on his robe, and headed towards Elazar's study.

The first thing he had to do was to extract the egg "*goo*", and dilute it into a drinkable form. That was the easy part. He immediately began meticulously contemplating his next move. As he walked by a framed mirror on the wall in the hallway, he could see his skin slowly returning to normal—a few strands of hair were sticking up from the top of his head.

Within an hour, Galax was his old self again, and had bottled the "*goo*" into a tiny vial and placed it around his neck. He was satisfied that he had figured out the first part of the mystery, and was now ready to eat a light lunch and take a quick nap in the room of orbs.

Before resting, he activated a large amethyst sphere to confirm that Elazar had made it safely to Talfryn.

Chapter Three
Wizards of the Kingdoms

ELAZAR and Mortighan were in the heart of Talfryn, walking along the streets of the city, taking their time as they passed by numerous traveling merchants, lodgings, and taverns, whose entryways smelled of cheap beer, old bread, and weary sailors. Elazar stopped and leaned over the rail of the bridge, gazing down at the faraway boats cruising by on the river below. It had rained rather hard that morning, and the refreshing smell of undergrowth and waterfalls were filling his nostrils like nature's body mist.

The streets were paved with colorful stones, and although noisy with activity, the sounds of market hagglers and musicians playing stringed instruments, were drowned out by the gathering crowd that was bustling into the main temple building.

Seventy-two wizards and enchantresses, all exquisitely dressed in fine robes with bright distinguishing garments, were piling into the enormous dome amphitheater, chatting vigorously among each other, making gracious gestures of salutations and various other greetings. Within minutes, Elazar and Mortighan had left the bridge, and were walking up the front passageway, heading towards their seats in the center of the arena.

There was a feeling of restlessness expressed throughout the members, while a couple of wizards caused a small commotion of animated outbursts. Several head speakers were murmuring compliments to their peers, and applauding as the eldest of them entered, and made his way to the front of the podium. He was a tall, lean, stern man, wearing a high hat, who pressed his lips together so tightly, his teeth chattered underneath his gums.

His name was Rufus Erwig, and after opening a thick book to a specific page, he looked through his spectacles at the large gathering, gesturing quietly to its members. Immediately there was a hush of silence as his slate-gray eyes glared upon them.

"Ah...hum," he said roughly, glancing about the place, "let us call to order our convention of the *Wizards of the Kingdoms* millennial festival. We have a long list of important proposals and issues to go over before our celebration this weekend. I hope you are all comfortable in your seating, and ready for this tedious task of preparing for the regeneration of our kingdoms for the betterment of tomorrow."

As he said this, many cheers and applauds were heard from the delegates. "Yes, yes, now simmer down. We are all anxious to hear what issues need our immediate attention, and what solutions are suggested to keep our planet from losing its peaceful course with us as inhabitants."

Elazar pulled out a small pad and ink writing instrument, preparing to take detailed notes of the proceedings. He was yearning to hear what every single member had to say about the past one thousand years of living.

"Enough said...I will now open up the floor for discussion, and allow our elders to speak their resolutions first," Erwig stated, as he moved to a nearby seat and sat down.

Elazar was seated near the front of the ring, on a wooden bench. He began drinking from a cup of *memory essence* that had been handed to him minutes after he had entered. He was happy to see such a large turnout. Smiling coolly at a passer-by—he stared gaily at the representatives from many continents and regions. A short, incredibly old, dwarf-sized elder stood up from his seat, and asked to be the first to take the floor with his commentary.

He hopped atop his bench, adding a few feet to his height, and calmly addressed the crowd, as everyone fell silent and listened. "Well," said the dwarf, clearing his throat. "I am very concerned about the extinction of numerous creatures of magic. Their eradication is causing a disruption in the flow of evolution. There are also many creatures in our kingdom that no longer exist. I'm afraid of the damage this will do, not only to our magic, but also to our peaceful environment."

The members of the assembly were in agreement, muttering in low voices to each other—eyes curiously transfixed on the wildly-bearded elder dwarf. Some had serious faces, and others seemed overly frustrated about the questions which were momentarily arousing their concern.

"I'd like to call as a witness, Illustra, the forest fae, *Queen of the Realm of Northford*," said the dwarf, as a winsome, green fae appeared. Her dress was like the forest itself, autumn leaves fluttering to the marble floor, as she nearly floated across the jam-packed auditorium. She had a very delicate face, and striking velvety eyes that gleamed from within. She was wearing a harvest crown made of foliage and branches, and had thick, flowing, maroon hair that was as lengthy and cascading as her gown.

"Our realms have been losing flowing waters from the streams, rivers, and lakes, which have all but dried up. Nature is being tampered with, and it is causing drastic changes in the natural order of life."

There was much commotion again, and Rufus Erwig hushed the members as quickly as he could, by rushing to the podium and waving his hands in the air. In reply, he said, "And do you know who has caused all of this tampering with nature?"

Elazar turned a deep, sympathetic ear towards the next delegates, who flew in from the lobby, soaring energetically about the summit. The language spoken by the swarm of ghostly sprites was unusually strange to understand, but most of the elders understood what was being said. One particularly gentle-spirited enchantress stood up, and translated their words for them.

"I have come all this way to warn you, and *I must tell you the truth*. My colony has been spying on these beasts for decades, as we both live in the same vicinity. They are *Troll* folk, living in the caves underneath the mountains, and they have been busy building a machine, which will alter our planet's eco-system. They grow more dangerous with time. I'm not sure who has ordered the creation of this contraption— giving them the help of magic that they do not possess. However, I do know that they are building up great heat from the volcanoes, and planning to use it to reconstruct our land masses."

"I have been paying special attention to the *Ember Trolls*," said Elazar unexpectedly; he rose from his seat, and everyone turned and gazed at him keenly. "I've seen what the Trolls are up to. They are definitely planning to move to the surface, and when they do, we must be prepared to live in co-existence with them."

Suddenly, there was an outpouring of melodramatic opposition, and one of the wizards roared, "Maybe we shouldn't allow them to *co-exist*. We should use our magic to make them *extinct!*"

"Yes, you're *right!*" cackled an unsightly enchantress, flinty eye's narrowing. Her white powdery face was caked-on like flour—lips and cheeks as red as rose petals.

"I agree...we *should* eradicate the beasts!" a stern-faced wizard admitted, nodding in agreement, and stirring up the crowd around him.

"Settle down, *settle down!*" bellowed Rufus Erwig. "We'll take that into consideration."

Elazar sat down, staring with grave frustration into the faces of all the members. He turned towards Mortighan, who gave him a quick smile, signaling his approval.

"Elazar is right. The Ember Trolls are planning something, and we must keep them under surveillance. I have even more information to reveal," Mortighan said flatly, to everyone's astonishment. "I am sure they have received orders from Madicon. I know this, because I've heard from the village towns-people that he has asked the Ember Trolls to eliminate all traces of the magical plants and species that we use for *medicines, cures, and remedies.*" Madicon, who was not in attendance, could not speak for himself, and so some of the council did not easily believe what Mortighan said.

"Yes, it is all true," said Illustra, rising to her feet. "I have sent my most trusted fae to ask the higher spirits for answers to many troubling questions. They have responded by giving us a *new prophecy.*"

"What is this *prophecy?*" Rufus asked, surprised.

"They say that our world is in terrible danger of mass destruction; that unless we gather to defeat them, many nations will be destroyed."

"Have your species been attacked?" asked the dwarf bluntly.

"Yes," said Illustra, feeling pain in her chest. "Many from my kingdom have been lost to the Ember Trolls. We have good reason to believe that they are in need of our elemental charms to complete their machine."

"What kind of *machine* is this?" asked an enchantress named Erma Grey.

"It is hidden from view. We have yet to discover its true location or function," Illustra expressed uncertain.

Elazar put his hands deep in his pockets, and cringed. He was remembering what he had seen on many occasions of astral projecting to the underground mountains. It worried him a great deal that the Ember Trolls were building this machine. He wanted to hear more about Illustra's problem with the magic extractions, but said nothing more to spark up the issue. He knew what had to be done.

A new topic was being brought to everyone's attention. After a moment, three sisters were standing side by side, radiating a brilliant blue hue, and talking in unison about their declining extra-sensory abilities. "We haven't been able to speak telepathically to our cousins, nor to ourselves. Our people are losing their clairvoyant powers. We're sure that in a few hundred years, we'll no longer be able to communicate this way," they all said in a high pitched voice.

Elazar was very interested in these three sisters, and started writing down notes in his journal book. He was writing energetically, when the rain began to build up outside.

The precipitation cascaded outside the towering windows, pouring down like showers of rushing rapids. After the droplets yielded, the air was wet and muggy, and a dark cloud covered the roof of the temple, giving the aura a sensation of a howling, angry wind.

The meeting went on for several more hours, and then broke for the evening, after which Elazar walked quietly out onto the balcony, and stood facing the vista. He gazed misty-eyed over the gorge, and far into the distance. He could see birds flying over a rainbow, and a tiny boat puttering by in the river that was about the size of a small ant. *There are so many problems that I don't know which ones are of the most importance*, he thought.

He was contemplating the millennial ritual that he had to perform, when he returned home to the castle. No one was aware of this secret tradition, none but he and Mortighan, who had now appeared beside him.

"There are some things I have been keeping my eye on. Nevertheless, this...this is definitely more than I assumed," Elazar said despairingly.

"I'm not in the least, confounded," Mortighan replied. "I expected you would have your work cut out for you."

"I've noticed more and more changes in the planet's eco-system. These are drastic changes. There is more damage than I realized."

"Yes, I can't believe that they are extracting our magic, and wiping out so many rare species." Mortighan sighed and shook his head. "I had *no idea* about that."

"I am keeping all these things in mind. Everything is of dire importance to me, so that I will be ready for the ritual when the time comes."

"Have you caught a glimpse of Galax?"

"I haven't felt any disruptions, since we've been here," said Elazar plainly. "I would have known it if there was something out of sorts."

"I'm sure he is doing a good job then," said Mortighan pleasantly, and in a tone that began to reassure Elazar.

"As long as he doesn't break the spell, the tower will be safe. Although, if he discovers what is hidden there, or the relics get into the wrong hands, we will have serious problems to contend with." After he said this, Mortighan gave him a reflective look that made Elazar nervous again.

An elder wizard came up to Elazar and spoke in a very feminine voice. "There are much more changes on Amunet from when we were young. Don't you agree?"

"It's not entirely the same, yes," Elazar responded, accepting a cup of cider from her.

"Of course, I haven't seen *a single* unicorn, nor have any merfolk been seen out at sea."

He glanced at Illustra, who was now standing behind them. Smiling mildly, he was taken in by the elegant flowers that were sprouting from her hair. She quickly bent down to pick up a diamond that had fallen from her eye, and placed it into Elazar's hand.

"A gift for you," she said.

"Thank you, Illustra," Elazar returned kindly.

"How is your sister Fortress doing?" he politely asked, trying not to seem too anxious for a response. He and Fortress were very dear friends. She had once helped him escape in battle when he was very young. Even to this day he was sure that she was the most skilled forest fae that he had ever known.

"Fortress has been working constantly. I worry about her. She is so concerned for the forest that she has not rested in weeks. She practices extreme magic that most of us don't dare to involve in. I just hope she knows what she's doing."

"If I know her," Elazar exclaimed, "she will do *only* what is necessary."

Mortighan had left them to their discussion, and walked away towards the refreshment table. He marveled at the magnificence of the statues of countless ruling ancestors, and the various fresco paintings of ancient historical events. Butterflies flew in from the balcony doors, and sailed upward, as far as the apex of the arena, and then trailed off towards the corridors that lead to the other specialty rooms.

By now, Mortighan was becoming quite hopeful. He greeted a young enchantress, and politely strode outside the grand temple, away from the five elders chatting fervently near the entrance. He stepped lightly into a magic shop called, *Magic Seeds and Beans*, and was greeted with cheer from the shop owner, whom he was well acquainted.

It was getting late now, and nightfall would bring a serious shiver, as did most nights in the elevated city of Talfryn. He and Elazar would have to get settled into their quarters before nightfall, and wait for the following day, which was when the celebrations would begin.

It was always a momentous occasion to see the streets lined with various tribes, races, and cultures from around Amunet. Dacey, the shop owner gave Mortighan a bag of fresh cocoa beans that he would later use to brew a pot of *magnetic* chocolate liquor.

With this drink, he would be able to gain more rhythm and dance better than anyone at the festival.

Once outside, he saw Elazar coming towards him, waving vigorously and holding a piece of parchment.

"We'll have to make a left on *Slantwise Road*, which is charmed by a spell that will make us walk *sideways*. Then we turn right on *Wind Chill Lane*, so make sure you're bundled up, and from there we go on a few blocks until we see the *Celestial Days Inn*. I've been given a map by a wizard, who highly recommends this place."

Elazar gestured readily at the faraway building near the corner of the map. "We'd better go, because I'll need plenty of sleep before I do my meditations," he suggested, folding up the map, and tucking it in his satchel.

"Ah, yes, I'm ready. I'm quite exhausted, and could use a good rest before morning. We've got a big day ahead of us—" Mortighan affirmed yawning.

Chapter Four
The Act of Vanishing

GALAX stood holding the liquid vial of "*goo*" from the armored-fish egg. He held his hand as steady as he could, while drinking a couple of drops of the now vibrant and glowing elixir. Sure that he had swallowed enough, he put his mind into the training he had been taught by Elazar. It wasn't an easy thing to do, keeping his thoughts focused on separating his body, and it drove him nearly mad just to shake inside himself, forcing his other half to divide on command.

Standing in front of the majestic metal door, he watched anxiously as his ghostly soul broke away from his physical body, forcing him to look in the face of his doppelgänger. Now an apparition, he passed his arm through the center of the glyph, moving his fingers around until he finally felt the vibrant translucent key. After he had pulled it out, he placed it into the right hand of his physical self.

Galax was ecstatic that he had uncovered the first mystery of the enchantment. He now held the key to one of three unbreakable seals. The second lock was going to be the most difficult, but he was sure he would be able to figure it out as he went.

The next test included *translating*. He was highly skilled at the expert task of stellar teleportation, but definitely thought himself a simpleton of inter-dimensional navigating. The *Liimer Star* had only shown Elazar vanishing, but had not given him a clue as to where he went in his travel. Translating required direction and focused movement into another dimension. He feared that he would never be able to calculate the precise location of where Elazar had gone.

Now that Galax had become one with his self, completely slipping back into his physical body, he put the key in his pocket and headed off to sit by the fireplace. The sun rolled down out of the sky, as the chilly night air began to creep in through the windows.

He thought about the places Elazar would have translated to. The ability to move in and out of dimensions impulsively was no easy achievement.

When he was a young boy grasping the basics of wizardry, it had taken him over two long weeks to master the skill. After he finally learned to translate into a spherical force field that Elazar had created for practicing, he spent more than a day vanishing constantly at will until he was tired.

Even weeks after his first attempt, he practiced every day, until he felt experienced enough to translate right out of the sphere, and into the dimension that Elazar had chosen for his first exploration. He had called it Zenith, and when he arrived there, he found loads of colorful plant life, some as alien to his home planet as he had ever seen.

The question still remained in his mind, of where Elazar had translated, and until he figured that out, he was stuck just idly holding the key. It was no use going any further with the quest until he was sure of where he needed to be.

Looking down at the key, which he had pulled from his robe pocket, he stared at it, admiring the advanced science, and the structure and lightness he felt in his hand. Then he remembered what Mortighan had told him about the magic of Delphi, and the fact that he had brought it from his own kingdom in another dimension. Delphi had translated back to that dimension many hundreds of years before, and left Elazar to protect whatever was hidden in the tower.

Galax was beginning to have a direction in his mind. He estimated that Elazar would have wanted to hide the second key somewhere ultra safe, and make it even more difficult to open the door, almost impossible if anyone but himself, of course, because he was good at getting into his master's head.

Now Galax went back to the door of the tower, and stood there, preparing to translate to Delphi's dimension. He didn't need to know exactly where it was in the universe to make it there safely. He only needed to be able to meditate on the whereabouts of Delphi, so speaking out loud, he shouted, "Take me to the wizard Delphi!"

A moment later and he felt a cold shiver ride up his body, and all his hairs were nearly standing on end. His eyes were blurred for several seconds, and he could not move his arms, legs, or neck, but after a moment, he was standing on the smallest planet in the discovery of planets. He knew it was tiny, as he could nearly see off the side of it. The ground virtually curved just over the horizon, which wasn't but a hundred yards from where he was standing.

In front of him was a deserted-looking, dilapidated wooden house. It was a one story building, made of decaying planks, with a small front porch. In the inside was a torn hole in the ceiling and from the backdrop of stars, the moon shone its light into the opening, causing rays of sparkles to streak the flooring.

He was almost too nervous to enter, wondering why such a small house would be sitting on such a diminutive planet. He was sure he could walk completely around the planet in less than an hour, and reach the house again. There were a few not-so-tall trees, and a nice bush or two, but after that, the place seemed empty, except for a creepy spider's web that was hanging from the porch rafters.

"Hello...is anybody here?" Galax shouted eagerly,

creating a pleasantly warm light orb. He had forgotten to bring along a lamp, or candlestick, for he had imagined it would not be needed. And now seeing that the moon and nearby stars were the only source of light, he figured his illuminating orb would have to do the trick, at least for a while.

He walked cautiously up to the front door, which was already ajar. The hinges made a creaking sound as he stepped closely, and looked inside the dark room filled with cobwebs and grimy furniture. He realized there was not much to the living area, but a dirty rug, a few pictures on the wall, a loveseat, and a bookshelf. There was nothing in the kitchen to eat, either. The dust rose up in his nostrils, so that he sneezed not once, but twice.

Galax knew what he was looking for. It was another key. This key would unlock the second lock, and it had to be protected, somewhere that nobody would think to look for it. He had quite a few questions running through his mind, wondering where Delphi was, and why he would be living on such an isolated and miniature world. If the key was there, and hidden somewhere, where would it be? He thought about this for a few minutes. He had gotten good at predicting the whereabouts of things, and considered himself a *natural* at tracing other people's steps.

This time though, he was completely mystified,

and had not a clue as where the key could be hidden. He went over to the stripped loveseat, and dusted off the cushions, coughing as a cloud of dust filled the air, and disintegrated into tiny specks and particles. He sat down, and glanced around the room, noticing the picture on the wall of Delphi and Elazar.

Elazar was younger than Galax had ever seen him before. He was probably around the same age as he was. He wore a colorful green robe and hat, and seemed to be cheerfully smiling, as if there was something significant about the moment when that picture was captured. Wizards had the ability to capture moments in time, and hold them in existence for as long as the memory was still remembered by someone, but once that memory was gone, the image would fade away, as if it had never been there.

Galax got to his feet, and began sorting through the books on the shelf. He found the first volume to be particularly heavy and wide. The title read, *"Diseases of the Netherworld, and How to Cure Them."*

The next few books were light and of no important interest. He had several volumes of *The Influences of Extra-terrestrial Wizards* back home in the study. However, there was one in particular that caught his eye, called *Changing Fate*. As soon as he grabbed it and pulled it off the shelf, the large decorative urn sitting next to it fell to the floor, breaking into several pieces.

The moment it shattered, Galax knew he had accidently disturbed the resting place of Delphi, and in the center of the ashes was a rusty metal key. As he picked it up, a ghostly figure rose from the remains, and spoke harshly at him, "How *disrespectful!*"

Slipping the key quietly into his robe pocket, he said, "I'm terribly sorry, I had no idea—" but before he could finish his statement, the ghostly figure flew at his face, and frowned.

"How *disrespectful...*young man! *Didn't anybody ever teach you not to mess with other people's belongings?* I'm not sure *you know who I am?* I'm the wizard Delphi, and I was resting peacefully until *you came along and woke me up!*"

"Sorrrrry...I didn't mean to," said Galax politely, trying not to trip over the rug, as the ghostly face seemed to be getting closer and closer to his own. Delphi was definitely not happy about finding him there.

"What are you doing, *going through my things?*" he asked.

Galax paused for a moment, and said, "I was looking for a book to read, as I have read almost every book on magic. And I was told by Elazar that you had a very unique collection."

Delphi's face turned from a frown to a look of amusement. He seemed to calm down a bit, and spoke more softly, "Elazar? I haven't seen him in a long time. In fact, I haven't had any visitors here in ages. No one to talk to, you see, so I've gotten used to sleeping."

The wizard Delphi was undoubtedly curious, floating around Galax with a bit of scrutiny in his eyes. He studied his facial expressions, while tenaciously looking him over.

"Most don't even realize I exist in this form, and are certainly unaware of my presence. You must be *special*, to be able see me, *I mean*. Are you a wizard... a pupil of my former apprentice, Elazar?"

"Well, yes, and I'm very gifted. I see many things that others can't," said Galax hastily.

"That's an exceptional ability, my boy," said Delphi, patting him on the back. "Now I have somebody to talk to. Can you spare a few decades?"

"Uh...well... I don't think so," said Galax alarmed.

"Well of course you can. I can tell you all about the trials and tribulations of my life, and how I ended up in this place. You see...it all started about twelve hundred years ago. Back when I was of a tender age, just like you, I had access to foreign knowledge that most wizards had never heard of. I was even best in my class of apprentices, and was considered as talented, as well...."

Galax sat down on the dusty chair, and listened to Delphi talk about everything from his childhood pranks to how he married a mermaid, and lived under the sea. He was starting to nod off a few hours into it, and finally began to wonder if he would ever get out of there. He presumed that Delphi wasn't planning on allowing him to leave any time soon. He then decided to come up with a plan to get rid of him, or at least to get back to his own dimension, without him noticing he had taken the key.

Then he remembered that Delphi had asked him how he could see him, and it gave him an idea.

He spoke suddenly, startling Delphi, who had been continuously talking, and was now on *how to keep faeries from reading your mind.* "Wait, don't go! Come back!"

"What do you mean, my boy? Are you able to see me?" Delphi asked.

"You're fading. I can barely make out your visage. I think I am not able to use my skills for too long."

"Oh, no, but can you hear me?"

*"What? Did you say something? I can't hear you anymore! Where...did you go? And I was just get-*ting into the story." He stood up, and started walking towards the door, as Delphi floated there, with a stunned look on his face. He watched Galax stride out to the front yard, saying, *"Delphi, are you there?"* A moment later, he had translated out of the dimension and back to his own study again.

Now he realized he had left the book on *Changing Fate,* but was too shaken up to go back and get it.

53

Maybe one day, he thought, but at least he had the key still resting in his pocket. He slipped his fingers over it, just for reassurance, and headed back to the study to unlock the seals of the tower.

He had two keys in his pocket, and was standing in front of the door again, grinning to himself, proud that he had made it thus far without being discovered. All he had to do was to follow Elazar's pattern, and everything would be revealed to him.

After repeating the words that he had heard Elazar speak, he placed the translucent key in the center of the transparent helix that appeared on the screen before him, and the first lock unlatched with a loud thud. He took the second key, the one from Delphi, out of his left pocket, and immediately unlatched the next lock noisily, after which he grabbed the corner of the door, and began folding it into a very small cube. The minute the cube was squarely in his hands, he placed the same metal key into the lock, and turned it slowly. Within a shimmy of a shake, he was standing on the other side of the tower, staring up at the huge ceiling.

Chapter Five
The King's Request

A HEAVY-SET bearded, overly dressed man sat highly on his decorated horse, and watched his troops assemble near the foot of Mt. Nova. The valley was strewn with slain soldiers for miles and miles, and the aftermath of defeat smelled of freshly spilled blood. For a moment, he observed a weary soldier drinking from his canteen, and after wiping his wounded cheek, he picked up his sword and shield, and headed towards the surviving men.

"I need to see Madicon at once!" shouted the angry leader, holding tightly to the reins.

"Yes sir, King Hasad. I will fetch him myself," replied Tobias, his commanding officer.

King Ismet Hasad stepped down from the horse,

and headed towards a large canvas at the top of the hill. The wind whipped his heavy royal robes around his ankles as he marched confidently towards the entrance, and then to a marble table where a long map was laid.

A moment later, a very tall, thin, dark-haired man entered the chamber, dressed in a black robe, and carrying a scepter in his right hand. He walked around the side of the table, and stood facing the king, who was staring angrily down at the map where little model soldiers were positioned.

"Madicon, I thought you told me your magic would prevent my troops from losing to Cassius. Now I have seen a turn in the battle, and we are losing more men than you predicted," he retorted, without bothering to raise his head to meet Madicon's gaze.

"I have not failed you yet, Ismet," protested Madicon. The king turned angrily towards him, and stared him directly in his eyes.

"Well then! What do you propose we do? I'll not have my forces be slaughtered by King Wyntir and his men!" the king screamed. "You promised to help me win this fight, and that is what I expect you to do, because if you don't, I'll have your head taken off your body and delivered to your enemies on a platter!"

Madicon swallowed hard as he realized he was losing favor with Hasad. It had taken many spells and enchantments to reach the status of *King's Mage*, and he wasn't about to lose his position. "I am working on a solution to this misfortune. Just give me time, and I will bring you the magic you request," he answered.

"You had better!" cried the king. "If I don't start seeing a change in this war soon, I'm holding you directly responsible."

The wizard Madicon fled the scene, his mouth turn downward; his eyes glowing a dark red hue, and went to his tent just a few feet away. He knew he had to think fast. He had exhausted his magic spells, and allowed the opposing side to gain momentum. He now feared that there was no solution to regain the king's trust, which he felt he well deserved. For all the power he had, would be useless without it.

While Madicon paced the dirt floor of his quarters, a few miles away, another king sat on his throne, and spoke seriously to his son.

"Nolan, my son, I am counting on you to take our army to victory. The last I heard, Kagen, your cousin, was defeating Hasad at the bridges of Yale, putting us at an advantage," Cassius Wyntir said, brushing his hand through his bristly beard. "We still have a chance then, to strike with force, and keep him from overthrowing our kingdom. They have set up camp many miles away in the mountains, but if they breach the outer walls, we will have no choice but to give in."

"Don't worry father, we will protect the kingdom.

I am riding out to the outer walls with my legion, to block them from coming any closer to Osnath."

Nolan Wyntir was a noble prince and good son to his father. He had been preparing for the opportunity to show his loyalty and strength, in the hope of impressing upon him that he would be ready to take his place when the time came. He knew that his father wasn't completely aware of the severity and brutality of Hasad's army. Their enemies would stop at nothing to reach Osnath, and conquer all the kingdoms in their path.

Nolan heard the patter of feet, and the heavy doors to the throne room were pushed open. A messenger was standing there—helmet in hand, with his hair tossed around his face—frowning deeply as the sweat rolled down his neck, and into his armor. "Kagen has sent me to inform you of Hasad's retreat into the mountains of Nova. He says that the king is planning to attack with a new weapon of some kind. The Ember Trolls have been building it, and there is no knowledge of what it is made for. He sends urgency, and hopes that you hasten reinforcements."

"Ride at once to my cousin, and tell him I am on my way. I will be there in time with my legion," stated Nolan.

"Yes *sir*," said the messenger, as he stepped out of the prince's way. Nolan immediately left the room. At the end of the hour, he was leading his men down the northern road towards the mountains of Nova.

As the time slipped away, Madicon grew more disturbed. He had been searching frantically for a new spell, trick, or some ancient magic that would turn the events of the battle in Hasad's favor. He had one old book that he had not used for enchantments, because of its age. The magic from its pages and times were believed to be legendary, and long gone from existence.

He flipped through the pages, becoming more and more enraged, until finally, he stood up, and tossed the book across the room. From deep within his eyes blazed up fiery red flames, peaking orange, until slowly fading into black again.

"There has to be something here that I am missing," muttered Madicon. He was now standing in an open area, away from any objects that might get caught in his way. It was not yet dark outside, but the sun was descending rapidly. *"Encrypto Scriptium,"* he said, and a moment later he had teleported to a place that consisted of many unknown treasures, records, and inscriptions that were kept in a private facility deep underground in the mountains of Nova.

The compendium was dated long before ancient civilization even began, and the language used to read the knowledge was as archaic as the existence of time itself. The elementals had kept this vault secret, and stood guard outside it day in and day out. No one was allowed to enter, except for those with the skill of teleportation, and no one with those powers even knew of its existence, except for Madicon.

The Troll elementals were aware of Madicon's entry to and from the chamber, and had allowed him access to the treasures, with the promise of magical help when they requested it.

Madicon opened several stone vaults that were inscribed with sacred geometric shapes and wheels. He pulled out a particularly large device, a nano sphere, and after it dropped from his hands, it immediately expanded to encircle his body.

Inside the sphere, Madicon meditated, recalling ancient wisdom. He sorted through documents that appeared in midair, lightly illuminating a vibrant blue hue, until he found something that struck his interest. It was an artifact that was supposed to have been formed at the beginning of creation, and if obtained, could cause the very foundations of reality to shift in any direction that the mind of the controller wanted it to.

Madicon was now convinced this object was what he was looking for. Although he hadn't seen anything like it during his lifetime, he knew there were some wizards old enough to have come across such magic, and it was possible that they were secretly harboring it from the rest of the world.

After putting the sphere back in its place, he

teleported himself out into the hills of Yale, and stood at the top of a valley, reaching out with his scepter, and saying a chant that summoned several dark creatures that could be seen climbing down out of the sky.

Bloodwyns were as creepy and as sunless as the midnight hour. They stood nine feet tall when perfectly upright, with long, slender, curved and pointed beaks that they used for ripping things apart, including flesh. They concealed themselves in the

shadows, hiding their half-bird, half-human bodies from the sight of onlookers, but they were sometimes glimpsed hovering over treetops, sailing ominously in the deep woods and secluded areas of the kingdom.

From the clouded sky, flew a flock of the black feathered beings. One of them landed rather close to Madicon, shading his smaller frame from the luminosity of the setting sun. His face was masked so that its piercing eyes could not be seen, and he transformed his plumed back into a dusky cloak and hood, draping over his figure like it was a part of him.

When they were all gathered before Madicon, eager to do his bidding, he generated an illusion of the artifact for them to see. A hologram appeared before their eyes, detailed and rotating 360 degrees for them to get a clear of a view as possible.

"Find it, and bring it to me!" Madicon roared urgently. "Search every corner, and every wizard, until you possess it. Don't come back without it! Go!"

The night had fallen, and the clouds had turned heavy with the fullness of raindrops. Shaking their accumulated mists, the water began to pour down.

Madicon had become drenched with wetness. He scoped the Bloodwyns as they stretched out their fringed wings in midair, one by one, racing towards the sky and into the gloominess of obscurity.

Chapter Six
Bloodwyn Trickery

STANDING in the center of the tower, Galax stared straight up towards the vaulted ceiling. He was fascinated with what he saw. It was cold and damp, and almost completely dark, except for a few glowing lights that lit up the stone wall in front of him. He walked up to the starlights that twinkled above, and grabbed a small metal cube floating just at arm's length. There were many strange cubes hovering all the way up to the apex.

Turning around to see what the other side of the tower contained, he shouted out a spell to brighten up the atmosphere, and a moment later, he was speechless. There, in front of him was a cluster of antique keys dangling in mid-air. There were as many keys as there were cubes.

"I can't believe this," said Galax, sighing.

The cube he had taken was intricately designed, and had a small keyhole in one of its faces. There was something so mysterious about the cube, that Galax was afraid to even contemplate just what kind of magic it possessed. He stared up again, studying the other cubes, and could see that every one of them had a different engraving; a distinctiveness. Each hexahedron held at its core a metallic sphere that touched all six sides perfectly. Using thermographic vision, he detected a heat source—a strange anti-matter—swirling inside the spheres.

Nervously, he took a key down from its spot, and put both items in the pockets of his robe. After a few moments, he teleported himself out of the tower, and was standing in the room of orbs again.

Galax didn't know what to do with the precious relics he had managed to obtain from the *Tower of Change*. In fact, he had no desire to tamper with the magic talismans at all. He knew he could accidently disturb the *fate of the world*, according to Mortighan, and he wasn't about to give Elazar a reason to come rushing back home from Talfryn.

He thought he would keep the items as mementos, and hide them in his room to examine, until he was ready to put them back again. He figured Elazar would be none the wiser, and would not notice a missing key or cube, since there had been so many of them.

So far, so good, Galax thought. Everything had gone according to plan, and he was feeling as contented with his progress, as he could be. "If Elazar could see me now, he would be fuming, but *impressed*," he said aloud, beaming with pride. "I can't BELIEVE I did it!"

Galax took the relics from his pockets, and placed them on a circular table. The table was draped with a beautiful green material that was thick and heavy, and patterned with golden stars. All twenty-two orbs had instantly activated the moment he had appeared, and now he was interested in a small citrine one that was sitting in the farthest corner of the room.

Galax believed that each orb had a special personality—a spirit entity, and if he held it closely, he could ask it a question, and it would respond. The orb was cold to the touch, and fit nicely in the palm of his hand. He closed his eyes, and concentrated on listening to any words, vibrations, or visions that the terrestrial sphere had to share.

"Hello Cynphonie, can you tell me about the item I am holding in my left hand?" he questioned.

"Yes I can. It is a cube of *fate*, and when unlocked, it has the power to *change the outcome* of things to whatever you desire." Its voice was high-pitched but intelligible; it seemed to echo in the recesses of his mind.

"Can you tell me how this is done?"

"You must imagine your fantasy, and it will alter your existence."

"Well, is there any risk, or special instructions I should know about?" he asked the orb.

"Yes, your consciousness is connected to the lives of others, so be mindful of what you mutate into this world. And remember, you can only use the cube once, and then all of its power will be transferred to a new reality."

"Like this, see?" As he heard these words, a vision came to him of dead trees and dry land that was drastically metamorphosed into a utopia of green plants, blooming flowers, and rich foliage.

"Thank you Cynphonie," said Galax to the orb, "I really appreciate your wisdom."

A dark shadow formed on the ground outside, as the wind blew furiously against the doors of the castle. It was the dead of night, and time seemed to be silent and motionless. A Bloodwyn appeared behind a tall tree, creeping slowly towards the only light seen coming from a window. It was on the second floor, where Elazar's apprentice lay resting in his bed.

Galax sat up, as a shadow crawled up his body, and when he opened his eyes, the overcast had vanished. He turned over in his sleep, and pulled the covers around his shoulders for warmth.

The Bloodwyn flew down to the front door, and morphed into a young maiden, elegantly dressed in a sophisticated gown made of velvet. Her silky straight, brunette hair fell softly down her backside. She smelled of a strong flowery scent, with lips of scarlet and blushed cheeks.

After straightening up her hair and wardrobe, she knocked hard on the door. A faint noise was heard inside, and then the doors were unlatched. Galax stood before her, with a perplexed look on his face.

"Can I help you?" he inquired.

"I'm so sorry to bother you, but I was on my way to Gregale to visit my sick mother, and my horse was stolen by passing thieves. I had to walk all this way in the dark, and I am so tired. Do you mind if I come in?"

"Well," he said hesitantly, cautiously considering her request. "I guess you can come in for a little while. Were you traveling alone? It is a bit cold out, and the forest is rather dangerous at night."

"Oh, I didn't mean to trouble you. I received a message that my mother was ill, and I didn't have time to ask anyone along. I just left the moment I heard."

"Oh, I see," he stated, leading her towards the

heat of the fireplace. "Please, warm yourself before you catch cold."

"Thank you. You are so kind," she declared. "I shall tell my father about you."

"What is your name?" he asked.

"Cameron."

"And yours?"

"Galax...Galax Hanz."

Cameron sat down in the chair closest to the fire, and leaned back, catching her breath. She gave Galax the impression that she had struggled strenuously to reach the castle, and was completely helpless and tired. Galax however, knew that it was a rarity to find such beauty wandering alone at night, and was very suspicious of her exhaustion.

He stared at her for a long time, and watched her take off her shoes, which were covered in mud. He could see her ankle just below her skirt, and when she caught him gazing, she just smiled sweetly and said, "Won't you come over here and talk to me for a while?"

She had such a charming demeanor that Galax just couldn't resist the invitation. He nestled close by the burning fire in a chair he usually sat in when Elazar was at home.

After she had surveyed the room, she asked, "Are you a wizard?" making her eyes dance with excitement.

"Well, yes, I'm studying to be one. I guess you can say that I'm pretty much one of them," he replied.

"Really! I've never met a wizard before. Can you show me one of your enchantments?" she exclaimed, practically begging him for a demonstration.

"Let's see," Galax murmured, contemplating what he should do. It had been a long time since he had done any whimsical enchantments, but he had an idea that he felt would make a great impression on her.

"Alright, I have one!" said Galax gleefully. He had to stand back. Stretching out his hand in front of him, Galax made a smooth wave through the air.

Fascinated, Cameron watched as the castle walls began to sprout vines in numerous places, as well as parts that were slowly disappearing to reveal a breathtaking forest with a large weeping willow tree maturing in the distance. Rays of sunlight lit up her face, and caressed her soft skin. A fraction of the room still remained, although it was covered in moss, vines, and other plant life. White lily flowers sprang up from the ground, opening their petals to scent the air with their sweet perfume.

The two of them walked towards the willow tree, just a short distance from the room, and stopped for a while under the branches that swayed gracefully in the gentle wind. Colorful butterflies danced around Cameron, lighting in her hair, and on her shoulder, and then flying away in a swarm towards the open sky.

Galax watched the look on Cameron's face, hoping that she was deeply moved by his enchantment; one that he had thought of just for her. He was beginning to be captivated by her, and since he had not been around many women in his life, it was easy for Cameron to glamour him with her magnetism.

"This is a wonderful charm, Galax," she said. "I had no idea you could do such a thing. You must be a very skilled wizard to be able to create such an illusion. It is so unbelievably realistic."

"You shower me with praises that I don't deserve.

I'm not as great as Master, Elazar."

"Elazar...This is his castle? Wow, I've heard many famous stories about him. You are lucky to be one of his students."

"Yes, I guess I am."

Cameron's eyes swept over Galax's wardrobe. She examined the shape of his bulging pockets, causing him slight alarm. She seemed to be shifting closer to him, enamoring him with her beguiling glare.

Galax moved swiftly away, drawing her back to the castle, and into their former reality.

"Can I offer you something to eat or drink?" he said, anxious to change the nervous vibe he was giving off.

She immediately grinned, and shook her head. "I would love some wine, if you can spare it," she said graciously.

"Sure. I'll go and get it then." He was beginning to warm up to her, admiring her beauty, and despite his resistance to trust her, he found himself enjoying her company, and even hoping they could become more acquainted.

Half afraid that something could go wrong, Galax went directly to the dining hall to remove the relics from his pockets. He had brought them down with him when he answered the door, and now he was beginning to wish he had put them away some place safe. Pausing, he gently pulled them both out, walked over to the elegant wooden table and set them down.

He wanted to stand there and admire the dimming light from inside the cube, but remembered he had to fetch wine, and that he had left Cameron alone, which he knew Elazar would not approve of. Almost completely mesmerized by the mystical talisman, he picked it back up, and stood there gazing into the darkness of the keyhole.

A long, blistered hand, displaying clawed fingernails, curled around the side of the open doorway behind him. Cameron had closely followed him, and was spying on his every move. The moment she had seen the cube, she had uncontrollably transmuted into her Bloodwyn form, inching the shadow of her winged arm towards the talisman with a beastly hunger in her eyes. Galax felt the darkness fall over his shoulder, and jumped, almost dropping the cube. In a flash he turned to face the doorway, which was now empty, and realized there was nothing there. He wasn't sure of what he had experienced, but decided he had better get the wine and return to his guest, before she became curious and wandered the castle grounds without him.

He set the relics down on the table surface, and using both hands to carry the glasses, he went back into the room and blinked at Cameron, who had drifted off to sleep. Not sure if he should wake her, or cover her with a blanket, he paused for long awhile, adoring her soft cheekbones and alluring features.

Silently she rested her face against the back of the chair, and then changed to a more comfortable position. *She must have been drained,* he thought, turning swiftly around to go up to his room for a covering. He had barely reached his bedroom door, when he heard a loud bump that stopped him dead in his tracks, chilling his insides with terrible dread.

The sound was coming from the front door, which was left wide open, banging against the wind, letting in heavy rain and sleet. The moment he realized the gravity of what had happened—he rushed outside just in time to see the Bloodwyn shoot rhythmically up into the sky, leaving a trail of black vapors in its wake.

Chapter Seven
A Change of Fate

His amazement at being deceived by Cameron, the Bloodwyn, weighed heavily on his conscience. Galax was now beginning to panic, because he knew Elazar would be furious with him. He backed his way into the front entrance, shutting the doors, and locking them, then turned and headed straight for the dining hall where he had left the cube and key. Stumbling back in shock, he affirmed they had been taken.

"Oh, NO...NO...This *can't* be happening!" he cried. "Elazar is going to KILL me!"

He was breathing uneasily, beginning to perspire, and frantically pacing the floor. There was no telling when Elazar would return, and he wasn't sure just how bad an effect the Bloodwyn could have on the world, if it tried to use the magic it now possessed. He was worried about the relic falling into the wrong hands, but for the time being, there was nothing to be done. There was no way to know how to find and retrieve the items. So, he knew he would just have to sit and wait until he could come up with an idea to the best course of action.

In the dark of night, an even darker mist could be seen falling from the sky. It was the Bloodwyn, and it was decending swiftly down towards Madicon, who was waiting restlessly outside the king's private canvas. Madicon was grinning from ear to ear as the Bloodwyn reached out and handed him the relics.

"Where did you find these?" he questioned, as he thoroughly examined the items.

"...in the castle of Sidonias Elazar. They were being guarded by his apprentice, Galax, whom I deceived," the Bloodwyn admitted, as it began altering its shape, and finally transforming into the maiden, Cameron.

"Elazar, you say? Hum, well good job, then. Are there any more of them?"

"I don't know, but I suspect there are many."

"I want you to go and gather the others. Once I have used up all its magic, we will need to comfiscate the other cubes and keys that are hidden in that castle. I will call you when I'm ready," commanded

Madicon.

"Yes, Master," said Cameron, as she shifted back into her Bloodwyn form, then took to the sky and disappeared out of sight.

Madicon held the cube closely to his chest. The wind was now blowing fiercely north, creating great movement in the thick of the trees. An owl flew by, and perched on a hanging branch. It turned its head towards Madicon, watching him with curiosity.

"Hoo... *hahoooo*..." it screeched.

Madicon's tall frame appeared inside the canvas, startling the king and the commander, who were quietly engaged with each other in deep conversation. As soon as Hasad saw Madicon, he immediately dismissed Tobias, and beckoned the Mage to come hither.

"I hope you have some good news to tell me," he said.

"Yes, I do. I have acquired a talisman that is powerful enough to change your fate. You will soon have your victory," Madicon replied, displaying the cube.

"Well, what are you waiting for then? Get to work, and make it happen."

"I intend to do just that!" confirmed Madicon. "There will be a major shift in the battle tomorrow that will help you regain your advantage. I plan on killing as many of his men as I possibly can. By midday, Cassius will hear of the tremendous loss of his army. Osnath will fall into your hands within a few days. I promise you."

"I knew you could find this—this, strange magic," he muttered, pointing to the cube. "I have every confidence in your success."

"Thank you, Hasad. I will leave you now," Madicon said, as he teleported himself out of the canvas.

The next morning, the army of Hasad was standing a good distance from their enemies. The day was overcast and humid. Both armies were gathered at the foot of Mt. Nova, ready for the battle to begin. Nolan Wyntir had not yet arrived with his legion, so Kegan rode his horse in front of his men, and asked them to do their best to protect the kingdom of Osnath.

On a large rock, high above the battleground, Madicon stood holding the ancient key and magic cube. He could see for many miles from where he was positioned, though his main focus was not on the battlefield, but concentrating on his desires for the triumph of his king.

Suddenly, there was a loud horn blowing across the grounds and far beyond. The soldiers on both sides began their charge, attacking each other with great ferocity and strength. Madicon held his vision for many minutes, and then proceeded to put the key in the lock of the cube, and turn it so that all six sides instantly faded away to reveal a vibrant sphere. He could feel himself being pulled into the center of it, as if he was being moved into another dimension.

The new dimension overcame the old one, replacing it with the birth of a new reality. A force of powerful energy and electricity came from the area where Madicon used the talisman, knocking some of the men that were a short distance away to the ground.

Madicon breathed a sigh of relief, as Hasad's army began to conquer and win. Swords blazed upon swords, clashing noisily into twisted metal. Arrows were shot from a far distance, accurately hitting their marks. King Hasad was quite thrilled, as he sat atop his horse, and surveyed the scene.

Many miles away, in a bar in the town of Talfryn, Elazar had felt a sudden jerk and pull of his body; it was a feeling he knew all too well. He immediately finished his beer, slapping the glass down hard on the table, and headed straight for the room that Mortighan was staying.

The look on Elazar's face was one of pure astonishment. He was sure that a *cube of fate* had been activated, and he was anxious to get home and protect the remainder of them. Upon entering Mortighan's room, he blurted out, "I must leave at once, Morti!"

"Why?"

"The tower has been compromised!"

"What? Do you believe it was Galax?" Mortighan asked tensely.

"I don't know yet, but I shall soon find out. I will teleport myself to the castle, and check on the status of things. I ask you to go into town, and find out anything you can. I will contact you soon," Elazar said, moving away from Mortighan. A moment later and he had vanished.

Galax was waiting in the room of orbs when Elazar appeared in front of him. He was afraid to tell him the story, for fear of his anger, but he spoke immediately and revealed the truth. "GALAX...*I'm very disappointed in you!*" Elazar erupted suddenly, telekinetically flinging an orb across the room and landing it delicately on the table near them.

"I know, and I'm *sorry*...if I hadn't been so curious, this *never* would have happened," Galax said shamefully.

"Never mind that—we've no time to lose, we must find out who's used the cube, and for what reason."

Elazar reached out and touched the orb, beckoning Galax to do the same. The color of the seeing device was crimson, and its personality reflected strong will-power and survival instincts. When Galax had placed his hand on its cold stone, the orb, whose name was Lootah, immediately gave them the vision of Madicon and the victory at Mt. Nova. To make matters worse, Bloodwyns were headed their way, and Madicon and a team of soldiers were also traveling by horseback, racing towards the castle at top speed.

Galax felt his stomach churn. He knew he had messed up pretty bad, and that Elazar would probably never trust him to watch over the tower again, but he feared the worst was yet to come.

"We have to go to the tower, NOW! The Blood-wyns will be upon us at any minute," Elazar commanded. "Galax, create a barrier to hold them off! I will work on reversing the spell on the tower doors. Once I'm in, I'll call for you." Elazar was acting with firmness and precise calculation.

Galax obeyed his master, and said a magic charm that formed a force field around the castle. This would hold off the Bloodwyns for a while, but only until Madicon arrived. After he had completed his task, he could hear Elazar call him telepathically.

Galax quickly teleported himself into the *Tower of Change*, and was baffled by what he was witnessing. Elazar had all the keys floating directly in front of him. They were turned horizontally, and wavering like arrows.

"Listen up, and listen well!" Elazar exclaimed. "I will disperse these keys to the four corners of this world, where no one but you will be able to find them. It will be *your* task to go and retrieve them, one by one."

"But...what about the cubes?"

"The cubes are useless without the keys to open them. I will remain behind, and protect them with my life. If something should happen to me, you are responsible for the magic in this tower."

"But...how will I know where the keys will be hidden?"

"I've created a special map that will point you to where each key is concealed in nature. You will need the help of a nature fae to assist your recovery. Seek out and find the one called, *Fortress of Northford*. I trust her."

Elazar handed Galax a velvet pouch that contained a metallic tetrahedron; a kind of pyramid.

"To activate the map, you'll need to first solve this riddle—the key to the truth is locked away like a mystery in a prism. The answer eludes you. When twilight comes, the dawn follows," Elazar said. "Can you remember that?"

"Yes, Master. I will remember."

Suddenly, there was a loud noise outside. The Bloodwyns had finally arrived, and were trying desperately to penetrate the shield.

"The Bloodwyns are here! How will I get pass them?" Galax was shaking and trembling with excitement. He had never actually been sent on such an important mission. He had always practiced his magic safely in the confines of the castle. Now he would truly have a chance to use his skills and training.

"I will open up a back way. Now stand aside, so I can disperse these keys before it's too late."

Galax watched anxiously as Elazar shouted *"quicktanicus"* and waved his hands. A passage manifested in the tower wall, leading to the south side of the castle. Immediately, the keys came to life, and like a flock of startled birds, they swiftly shot through the opening, and flew off in different directions. Galax stood at the exit, and watched the keys vanishing. Then he headed outside after the last one had disappeared. Outside, the shield was still holding strong, and although each key had secretly passed through it effortlessly, on the north side of the castle, the Bloodwyns were still trying unsuccessfully to break it down.

Taking his horse from the stable, Galax rode away as fast as he could towards the north to find Fortress the nature fae.

After all of the keys were safely dispersed, Elazar marched steadily out of the tower. The open doors swung shut, and telekinetically locked behind him with a loud thud. When he had reached the front entrance, he could see Madicon dismounting his horse, and preparing himself to penetrate the shield with a spell.

Madicon raised his scepter, and a red electrifying light shot out from the end, causing a rupture in the lining of the force field's wall.

Elazar was poised readily at the breach, boldly waiting for Madicon and his men to enter.

Chapter Eight
Sphere of Entrapment

IT was getting late, and while he pretended to be mentally collected, Galax felt humiliated. He thought about how greatly he had messed up the most important task he'd ever been given. Elazar finding out that he had broken the spell on the tower's door was one thing, but allowing the mysterious magic to be snatched up and used by an evil Mage was another thing entirely. He knew he had to prove himself worthy again, and the only way to do it was to retrieve the keys, bring them back in one piece, and not allow Madicon to get his hands on one.

The first thing on his agenda was to find this nature fae, called Fortress. He was galloping heavily on his stallion, and after he had gone a good ten miles away from the castle, he reached a fork in the road. He coaxed his horse to slow down so he could take another look inside the velvet pouch that Elazar had given him.

Dismounting, he walked over to a tall signpost. Opening the pouch carefully, he brought out the metallic tetrahedron, and held it up to the light of the sun so he could glimpse the details of the letterings. He had no idea what he was looking at, but he was absolutely sure that this was a mechanism from the stars. He had heard legends about artifacts and talismans given to his ancestors by visitors from another world, but he had never before laid his eyes on one.

Now he was holding a sacred object in his hands, and had been given the authority to use it. The small pyramid was heavy, and so he placed it tenatively back in the pouch, looked at the signpost, and mounted his horse again. There were two directions, and he wasn't sure which one would lead him towards Northford.

Strapped to his waste was a regular scroll map, securely tucked away in a leather tube. For a moment he glanced back towards the castle, wondering how Elazar was scoring against Madicon. He was concerned that he wasn't there to help him protect the tower, but he knew from years of experience that Elazar could hold his own. Besides that, it was the first rule of an apprentice to follow his master's instructions, even if he didn't always understand what was being asked of him. Elazar was wiser and older than he was, and if he had asked him to lay down his own life, he would have trusted him entirely with it.

Finding Fortress was going to be a long and treacherous journey, according to the map, which he was now studying diligently. Once he was there, he would have to convince her to follow him to the ends of the world. *Now, I wonder how I'm going to do that,* he thought.

Taking the reins in his blistered hands, he cued his horse, and trotted down towards the nearest path that lead to the small village of Zindel.

The moment Madicon broke the magical force field protecting the castle, Elazar flew at him a basic stifling spell. *"Percuralyzsus!"* he yelled unexpectedly, waving his hands. He had left his scepter behind, convinced that it would slow him down.

Madicon was immediately stunned and thrown a few paces back. Before Elazar could stop them, several Bloodwyns began flying towards him, blocking him from having a straight shot at Madicon. While Elazar focused on electrifying two of them with a shockwave, Madicon regained his movement, and cleverly teleported himself inside the castle.

To his horror, the door to the tower had been sealed shut. He knew he had no way of knowing what spells Elazar had used to keep it secured. There was only one thing left for him to do. It was either Galax or Elazar that he would have to get to open the tower. And he knew that Elazar would give up his life. Galax Hanz, however, would be easier to persuade.

Outside, Elazar had managed to obliterate several Bloodwyns and reseal the force field. At least for a while, he would be able to prevent any more of them from entering the grounds. His next move was to have it out with Madicon.

Madicon gradually turned, facing Elazar, who had just teleported himself behind him.

"What! Did you think I would have left it wide open for you?"

"No...not at all, Elazar! I knew you were too clever to allow *just anyone* to enter, so that is why I came prepared," Madicon said smiling.

"Well, is that so? You can try it, but you'll never get in the tower!" Elazar warned.

"I don't plan on it. Not without GALAX!" Madicon exclaimed, red flames alighting in his eyes.

Before Elazar could think—nonetheless move, Madicon was aiming a very powerful enchantment at him. It was a spell he had never heard before. There were many spells that were unique to the area of study a wizard was interested in. But this incantation was different. It had a foreign sound to it. It was the kind of magic that was not from this world. He felt somewhat taken aback by the words Madicon was saying, and yet, it sounded all too familiar to him.

"*Yaves san asa murotto...transporto entraptium trilustralis—*" chanted Madicon.

"Where have I heard this spell before?" he asked himself. "I know it, yet I can't quite...."

"*Silenscio!*" shouted Elazar, before Madicon had completed his last word.

"*Secretum!*"

Elazar was a moment too late. Madicon had released upon him an ancient curse that was literally spellbinding. It was like nothing he had ever seen before. His vision was momentarily blurred, and he felt a gust of wind forcefully hit his backside. He wondered where he was. The scenery had changed so drastically, that he felt a moment of bewilderment.

He could see an unending field of flowers, and a cloudy sky. The air was fresh, and yet, he could still see Madicon, but when he tried a rebound curse, he felt it being thrown back at *him*. The closer he got to Madicon's image, the farther away he felt he was getting to him. This was no ordinary trick.

"What is this?" Elazar screamed irritably.

"*The Sphere of Entrapment!*" Madicon hollered, laughing wickedly. "You are bound in there for the next fifteen years, old man. And there is nothing you or anyone else can do about it. This sorcery came from before this world was made."

"I will find a way out, and when I do—" Elazar hissed.

"When you do, it will be too late for you to stop me!" Madicon exclaimed. "I will hunt down Galax, and use him to gain access to the tower."

"You may have trapped me for now, but you can't prevent me from helping him," Elazar grumbled.

"Try as you may, but I'll have my talismans!" Madicon roared. "The closer you get to him, the farther away you'll become," he laughed. "You might as well take your time, because you'll be using up all your energy just to stay alive in there. You have no idea what power has enslaved you. I guess you'll figure it out soon enough."

Elazar stood very still. He knew that Madicon was right. He really didn't understand the curse that had captured him. He would have to be careful, just in case there were any more surprises. In the meantime, he set his sights on contacting Galax to warn him that Madicon was coming after him.

Miles away, on the outskirts of the small village of Zindel, Justise, a warrior woman, had laid in the grass, resting her head on a rock. She was tired from her enduring pilgrimage towards Talfryn. She was going there to find her uncle, her only remaining relative, whom she had been told was a *wizard* of the Kingdom.

Justise closed her eyes, and immediately she saw a vision. A Bloodwyn was waiting in the dark shadows of the forest, hiding behind a tree, preparing to attack a traveler that was about twenty miles down the path from where she was resting. She was used to having sudden visions. It was a talent she inherited from her enchantress mother, who was now deceased.

As she searched her vision, she saw that the young man was singing, and after a short while, he levitated a large downed tree branch that was blocking his path. After she realized he was a wizard, she was immediately anxious to contact him. She assumed he would be headed towards Gregale, and on to the *Wizards of the Kingdoms* festival, and might be able to help her locate her long lost relative.

She hastily gathered her belongs, which wasn't much; a sword, a short knife, and a pair of boots, and mounted up her mare who was eating grass nearby. As fast as she could, she raced towards the traveler, to see if she could help him before it was too late.

Galax hadn't picked up any signals that he was being followed. He hadn't heard any voices in his head, or even received any telepathic messages from Elazar, which he was sure he should have received by now. This was worrying him. Despite his concern, he kept in good spirits, and continued on the path towards the village.

Justise was riding with anxious speed now, and as the sun began setting, she was worried that she would not be able to reach him in time. The Blood-wyn had perched itself up in a tall tree, and was about to swoop down and attack Galax at any moment.

Elazar was concentrating on sending Galax a message. He tried many times to release himself from the sphere, but it only made matters worse. With each use of his powers, he felt more and more exhausted. The sphere's energy force seemed to be draining his powers, storing it up to be used against him. Elazar thought he had only a few chances to use his telepathy, and so he resolved to use it when he absolutely needed to.

Sensing Galax was walking into an ambush; he concentrated, and spoke softly to him.

"Galax, you must listen," he said. "Madicon has entrapped me in a force field that I am unable to break away from. You must protect the keys with your life. Do not let him gain access to the tower, no matter what the cost. I will find a way to release this curse."

Galax gained control of his now uneasy stallion, as a projected figure of Elazar appeared. After he listened to what was being said, he answered him. "But Elazar, what if I need you? I'm not sure I can do this."

"You must!" said Elazar. "You have been entrust-ed with the most important mission of all. The fate of the world is in your hands now. I can do nothing to help you. You must use all you have been taught, and do your best to put things right. I will contact you again when I am able."

"Yes Master, I will try my best."

"And remember, you must not let Madicon have access to the tower. Do everything in your power to stop him," Elazar instructed.

A moment later, he was gone. Galax was shocked, worried, and nearly panicking again. He was on his own now, and he was sure he was not ready for what trials he would be facing.

Sugar Cane, his white horse had suddenly jerked back, and made a frightening squeal. For some unknown reason, he refused to go any further down the path.

Galax tried to coax him onward. "Whoa, Sugar, it's okay boy. Let's go, he commanded," petting the side of his thick neck.

Sugar Cane only bucked harder, and turned the other way, speeding out of the vicinity. He bucked so hard, that Galax fell off and rolled on the ground.

He could see the backs of Sugar Cane's hooves as he hurriedly disappeared out of sight. Galax stood up, dusting off his clothes. He stared down the dark and shadowy path leading to Zindel. The night had just swung down out of the sky, and the trees seemed to be thicker, and heavier than usual.

He thought he caught sight of a dark figure flying by a few feet ahead of him. *"What was that?"* he said aloud. Curiously he began walking towards the spot where he had glimpsed the distraction. With slow and precise steps, he inched closer and closer down the path. All of a sudden, a flurry of wind stirred up a pile of bright orange and yellow autumn leaves, brushing up against his feet.

With a sharp slash, the Bloodwyn swooped down and sliced Galax's upper arm, cutting a small hole in his sleeve. Galax was caught off guard, stumbling back in pain, as he realized he was bleeding from the shoulder. He grabbed his shoulder, and moved rapidly out of the way as the Bloodwyn again tried to slash a hole in him.

The Bloodwyn's cut was poisonous, and within minutes, Galax felt himself getting weaker. He could hardly keep his thoughts together, as everything around him slowly became a faint blur. His sight was growing darker, and his arm burned with intensity. He felt his knees buckle from under him and completely give way. After he had fallen to the ground, he laid there helpless. The Bloodwyn approached him, standing over him with anticipation of his blackout.

Before Galax lost total consciousness, he heard the Bloodwyn scream out in terror, as a sharp blade came out of nowhere, and punctured his midriff. The Bloodwyn jerked horrifically this way and that, screeching like a wild animal, until he took his true form—the body of a dead man.

Galax woke up from his sleep, dazed and confused about what had happened. It was now daylight, and he could see that his wound had been carefully attended to. He jumped suddenly when a hand reached down and touched his shoulder.

"Who are you?" he asked.

"Be still. My name is Justise," she said, as she peeled away the leaf from his skin, and checked for further bleeding.

"What happened back there?" he questioned. "Did you kill the Bloodwyn?"

"I released it from its agony, if that is what you were wondering."

Galax looked at her skeptically. She was an exceptionally tall woman, muscular, yet lean, and seemed very skilled at healing medicines. He could tell by her warrior's attire that she was no ordinary woman.

"Well, aren't you going to thank me?" she snorted.

Galax frowned. He was still unsure if she could be trusted. "Why did you risk your neck for mine?" he asked.

"Well, because...I need your help."

He was sitting up now, paying close attention to what she was saying. "What do you want?"

"I know you're a wizard, and I was hoping you would help me find someone."

"Whoa, wait just a minute. I didn't ask you to protect me," he roared. "I was doing just fine without you."

Justise laughed at him. "Right," she said sarcastically. "*Whatever*—" She fidgeted with her knife, and then placed it back in its carrying case.

Galax thought about it for a moment, and then calmly asked, "Who is it you're seeking?"

"It is a wizard by the name of Mortighan Remus Shalshank."

"Morti?"

"Wait, you *know* him?"

"Well, kind of...what do you want with him?"

"I have an important message to deliver. How do

you know him?"

"He and my master are good friends."

"Well, actually, he's my uncle," Justise proclaimed.

"*Right*—" said Galax, shifting his eyelids towards the sunrise. A hawk flew by and landed on Justise's shoulder.

"Nellie, you're back. Good girl," she said, feeding the hawk a treat, after which she turned and looked at Galax, who was eyeing her curiously.

"No...really. I need to find him as soon as possible."

"Well, you're out of luck, because I'm on my way to find someone myself, and I haven't the time to be taking a side trip."

"But I thought—" Justise replied.

"You thought that because you rescued me, that it would ensure I would help you."

"Well, yes...I did."

"Under normal circumstances, you would be right, but unfortunately, my mission is especially imperative. I'm in a hurry...so I can't help you."

"Which way are you going then?" Justise asked.

"Why, are you planning on following me?"

"It depends."

"Hey, how did you know I was a wizard, anyway?" Galax questioned. "I never told you that?"

"I'm clairvoyant, that's how. I saw you headed

towards the Bloodwyn, and I also saw you perform that enchantment on the road."

"Oh, I see." He was scratching his head now. Perhaps he could use a clairvoyant warrior. He might need her abilities to help him fight the Bloodwyns— if they came back for more—and he was sure they would. He observed her brave demeanor, and could tell she was definitely capable of protecting him.

"Well, I might be able to help you, but I'll have to find my person first. Then we will see what I can do."

"Where are you headed exactly?" she asked.

"I'm looking for a forest fae that goes by the name of *Fortress of Northford.*"

"*...a forest fae*? I'm sure I *don't* want to know what that's all about."

"It's a long story, but if you agree to watch out for me so I can reach her safely, I'll do my best to help you find Morti," he vowed assuredly.

"Good, then we had better get moving. North-ford is a *long* ways from here, my friend. I know a shortcut, but it'll still take us a good while to get there." She mounted up, waiting patiently while Ga-lax feebly stretched out his legs.

Flapping her sturdy wings devotedly, Nellie flew serenely up into the sky, at Justise's request, in search of the wizard Mortighan. Galax whistled his usual call to summon Sugar Cane, and a moment later, they were speeding off together towards Northford.

Chapter Nine
Fortress Agrees

BY nightfall, Galax and Justise had reached the valley of Mesniel. The wide hollow was shrouded in a rich blanket of twilight, and the smell was sordid. Justise slept for a long while, but Galax sat down under a tall tree, and stared at the pyramid map, wondering if he would be able to figure out the answer to the riddle that Elazar had told him. Justise mumbled something under her breath, and stirred restlessly in her sleep. When she finally awoke the next morning, Galax was cooking a pigeon in the fire, and watching her intently.

"What was all that mumbling about?" he asked.

Justise turned towards him and frowned. "What do you mean? What mumbling?" she replied.

"You must have had a really bad dream, because you kept saying something about the beasts changing everything. What beasts were you talking about?" he questioned, handing her a bowl of meat.

Justise's face fell blank, as she tried to recall her dreams.

"Yes, I remember now. I saw an army of beasts, and they were building a machine."

Now, Galax had a blank look on *his* face. He was chewing on his food, which he quickly swallowed, and then said, "What sort of machine?"

"I don't know exactly, but it is not a good sign. I have a bad feeling that this is one of the visions my ancestors has sent to warn me of the coming of the destruction of our world. My people believe that a major catastrophe will cause our lands and seas to shift drastically, altering our geography, destroying our ability to co-exist with the creatures of this world."

"I've never heard of it." He drank from his canteen.

"This is the reason I must speak to Mortighan, as soon as possible. He is meeting with the *Wizards of the Kingdoms*, and I need him to deliver the message. We are running out of time, Galax. He knows about the beasts in the mountains; many of the high wizards know of their existence, but they have yet to do anything about it."

"Well, I can see this is a very important mission. You should never have stopped to save me from the Bloodwyn."

"My instincts told me to do it. It assured me that you were a part of all of this, and that I needed to help you. So I did." She smiled at him, letting herself feel a kinship for a millisecond before her face turned serious again.

"I do have an imperative task to attend to. You're right about that; however, I'm not sure I can help you on your quest. You see, I am in search of the nature fae, *Fortress* to help me retrieve the powerful magic that will keep our world from being restructured by an evil Mage called, Madicon."

Justise was quiet for a long moment, as she thought about what Galax had said. For some reason she felt there was a definite relation to his mission, and the message *she* was trying to deliver.

"Wait! I think we should work together, you know, as a team. My senses tell me we are important to each other. I don't know how I know. I just do. You'll just have to trust me on this, because I'm coming with you."

"What about your message?"

"There's time. I will deliver the message while we find this power you speak of. I'm sure there is a connection to the beasts and their machine."

"Well, if we can find this forest fae, maybe she

can help you deliver your message. Nature fae are powerful telepaths, you know. We might be able to ask Morti for help, too."

Pointing to the river below, Justise whispered to Galax to keep quiet. She stood up and quickly moved towards the edge of the valley, so she could get a better view. A legion of armored men could be seen following the river, riding swiftly towards Romenel, the nearest major township.

"They are carrying the black and gold flags of Osnath," Justise muttered.

"Osnath, but why are there so many of them?"

"They must be going to war."

Justise felt a sudden pang in the pit of her stomach. An abrupt jerk took her mind away from what she was witnessing, and expanded it towards the terrain, until it rested on the Mountains of Nova. There, standing on a cliff, she saw a Mage holding a talismanic cube, conjuring up a spell that she was sure was apocalyptic. Her vision rested on Madicon for 30 seconds before flowing outward again and magnifying over a battlefield of soldiers, and then into the caves below. Underneath the mountain, she watched the beasts adding parts to their diabolic machine, and immediately realized it was the one she had dreamed of many times before.

"Justise? Justise—" Galax waved his hand in front of her face, until she snapped out of her trance.

"Did you see anything?"

Justise nodded assuredly.

"What was it?"

"I was right! The Mage you called Madicon, is in league with the beasts of Mt. Nova. I saw the legion of Osnath fighting in the canyon below him. They were losing. We have to hurry, before Madicon gets control of Osnath."

"Osnath... Why does that place seem so familiar to me?" said Galax, searching his soul for answers.

He was remembering something...

A vision of himself as a baby playing in the courtyard, resurfaced in his mind. There was a gracious woman there, and he knew she was his mother. She had long flowing white hair, and an aura of purple light vibrantly lit her hands and face. He felt warm and happy in her arms, as she picked him up and held him lovingly.

Galax had always wondered who he really was. From early childhood, he had been raised by Elazar, who never spoke of his family or where he had come from. He didn't say anything to Justise about his strong attachment to Osnath, or what he was experiencing. He resolved to keep these emotions of familiarity to himself, supposing it wasn't the right time.

"We have to go!" said Justise with a sharp tongue. *"Now!"*

She seemed shaken up a bit.

"Alright!" Galax shouted, mounting Sugar Cane. "I'm right behind you!"

The two of them carefully rode down into the dale, following the waterway, like Osnath's army had done. It was evening when they reached Romenel—a ghost light flickering on the tavern post, was beckoning them to enter.

Inside the somewhat crowded *Beer Tree Inn*, Justise asked Galax, "I thought wizards could teleport themselves anywhere they wanted to?"

"Yes, we can, however, I brought Sugar Cane with me, because of the forest of Northford. You see, there is no way I can get into Northford by teleporting. Fae are powerful beings, and they use enchantments to prevent us wizards from using magic in their territory."

"Oh, I didn't know that," muttered Justise, "So how are you planning to even get near these fae then? I've heard many tales that their villages are usually well hidden."

"I don't know yet, but we'll figure it out when the time comes."

The fire was burning warmly on the hearth, and Galax sat at a round table, suspiciously eyeing the doorway. He was still nervous about the Bloodwyn attack, and feeling an eerie sensation in his bones. Justise engaged herself in a friendly conversation with one of the locals, whom she felt was very welcoming and informative.

Expectedly, a couple of weary Osnath soldiers strode into the pub, and sat down at the bar. Galax rose up from his seat, following close behind them, with the hopes of eavesdropping on their conversation.

"I've heard that King Hasad is in control of a very powerful Mage. It doesn't look like we have a fair chance in this war, even with our bravest men on the frontlines," said the blond-headed soldier, raising his tankard for a sip.

"You're right. We're most likely walking into a trap, and I'll bet Prince Nolan won't turn us around, even if he knows we're all going to die. He'll have us fight to the death," said the other soldier.

"Awe, I'm agreeing with you...Keith. We may as well send messages back to our wives, of our loving farewells," the blond one smirked. The two of them drank their beer, and walked back out of the pub towards their horses.

Galax came back to his table, where Justise was waiting curiously, and sat down abruptly.

"You know, I think this prince just might come in handy," said Galax.

"What prince?" asked Justise, smiling with interest, "How do you figure?"

"Prince Nolan of Osnath. He is very brave, and courageous. If we can impress in him the serious nature of this war, we may be able to encourage their victory."

"I'm not sure I'm following you," Justise uttered in a low voice.

"All I'm saying is that we could possibly use his allegiance."

"Perhaps you are right, but we need to be careful—no matter what. We can't trust anyone," Justise warned. Galax nodded in accord.

There were no sounds in the forest of Northford. The air was still, and the area was silent and foreboding. They had both eaten breakfast early, and traveled on horseback before sunrise towards their destination. In the thicket of bushes and tall trees, a few birds flew by, circling the sky ominously. It reminded the apprentice of the Bloodwyns, creating a penetrating knot in the pit of his stomach.

They had been riding their horses for about an hour, when Galax decided to dismount Sugar Cane, and go the rest of the way on foot. He needed to locate the entrance to the hidden village, and to do so, he would have to pay close attention to the particulars of the forest.

"I believe we are nearing the village," he said, examining the pinkish aura of a leaf. "I can feel it. The energy is vibrant nearest this trail."

"What trail? I don't see anything," Justise questioned, searching the ground.

Galax stared ahead, and with a simple wave of his hands, the path magically revealed itself.

"This way," he said.

"Oh, I see....you go on ahead, and I'll follow you," Justise gestured.

Galax stepped cautiously down the beaten path, images of Elazar flashing through his brain. He could have used his help now, but there had been no more communications from him.

Without word, Justise knelt beside an enormous tree, and plucked a large orange flower from its branches.

"I have seen these flowers before. We must be really close," she said.

"Why do you say that?" Galax asked, wiping the sweat from his face with a worn cloth.

"These are called Cateras. They are exceedingly rare, found only in places that have been changed by enchantment," replied Justise.

"How do you know this?" Galax asked, studying the flower warily.

"I once traveled with a wizard who carried with him an elixir. It had a scent like no other. He said it was made from the petals of Catera blossoms, and he showed one to me. He claimed that this fragrance was used to awaken the senses to that which could not be normally sensed. I did not know what he meant exactly, but I remembered the flower and its aroma, very well."

Galax reached up and picked a Catera from the tree. "We could use this," he said, breathing in the sweetness of the aroma. "I have a feeling it will help us find their village."

Justise nodded, and carefully pulled down several of the flowers that were above her.

There was a noisy cracking sound that startled Sugar Cane. He went galloping precipitously in the opposite direction from whence they came, as Justise's horse stepped back a few feet, unsteadily, and then disappeared through the forest behind him.

Galax hesitated. He stuffed the flowers into his satchel, and listened.

"Did you hear that?" Justise looked around cautiously.

"*Shhhh!*" he gestured.

He was sure he had heard a rustling noise coming from a few feet in front of him. Justise swiftly drew her sword, and they both walked slowly towards the reverberation. They had come several paces within the thick of the forest and halted. The woods were oddly quiet again. A large red cloak was spotted, moving pass one of the nearby trees. It glided silently back and forth and quickly jolted out of sight.

Justise was fast, running towards the flowing cloak, which had unexpectedly emerged from behind a wide tree, while Galax stood glaring in disbelief and watched.

The cloak floated several feet above them, waving back and forth in a slithering sort of way. Justise reached out to grab it, and was immediately flung backwards, and unto the ground.

As if spooked, the cloak ducked down, and whizzed pass them, flying out of range.

Justise sprang forward, following close behind. She was breathing heavily now, and calculating how soon she would catch up to it.

"WAIT!" Galax blurted.

"What?" Justise shouted. Panting, she turned around and stared at him. The red cloak stiffened, hovering aimlessly in mid-air. The back of its tail blew fiercely about, as the wind whipped at it abruptly.

"We mean you NO HARM!" Galax shouted. "We are looking for the village of Northford. Can you help us?"

"What's the matter with you?" Justise retorted, staring dubiously at Galax.

"Trust me....it's a *ghost!*" Galax said, tensely.

"Are you sure?"

"Yes, I'm sure." Galax replied. "Take a long whiff of the Catera, and you'll see."

"Oh, very well then," Justise nodded, frowning skeptically. She didn't believe what Galax was saying, but trusted his judgment. Taking a deep breath, she allowed her nostrils to fill up with the aroma that the Catera was releasing.

As Justise's senses awakened, she stared at the cloak distrustfully, watching the ghostly face of the dead man appear. It was a tall, slender man. Although slightly decaying, his handsome white face glittered with light. He was dressed like a rich merchant of the sea, and in his blackened eyes were the reflection of deep pain and suffering.

Justise skillfully swung around her sword, preparing herself for attack. She didn't trust the ghost, who was still floating silently in midair, glaring down at them, curiously. His face was stern, and calculative.

"How did you know?"

"I can see ghosts easily," Galax said. I learned that I had the talent, just before I came on this journey."

"I don't like him," Justise blurted out, suspiciously.

"Well, from the way he keeps looking down at you, I don't think he likes you either," Galax agreed.

Angrily, the ghost flew at Justise. She stabbed him straight through his heart. Before Galax could move in, the ghost grabbed her arm, and dragged her away, kicking and screaming.

"Justise! Justise!" Galax yelled, running frantically after them, but it was too late. The ghost was long gone, leaving Galax standing alone in wonderment.

Without delay, he pulled the Catera blossom out of his pouch, and concentrated heavily, nearly burning a hole in one of the petals. Less than 30 seconds later, he was holding a glass bottle of elixir.

Taking the top off the cap, he sniffed the perfume several times. His vision blurred for several moments, and his heart began to beat violently. As the beats slowed down, he started to see a vibrant light coming from just beyond the nearby trees.

Everything was warm and fuzzy now. The leaves on the trees were sparkling with a rainbow of colors. Light seemed to be pouring down from everywhere. It was almost blinding.

He walked leisurely for a mile towards the brightest colors, until he saw a large shimmering crystal, positioned on the grassy moorland.

"This must be the entryway to the hidden village," he said aloud, walking towards the crystal. Sure enough, he was able to walk into the center of it, and come out into a plush garden.

There, as if waiting patiently for his arrival, was an agelessly beautiful fae. She was slimly built, and wore a colorful gown. Butterflies flew around her, lighting in her wavy blond hair. She smiled serenely, and beckoned him to follow her.

They passed a noisy waterfall, after which she spoke softly. "Hello Galax. My name is Nimika. I will take you to Fortress. She is expecting you."

"Please, I need to find my friend. She was taken by a ghost. We must hurry," Galax pleaded.

"It was the Ghost of Northford. She'll be alright. Fortress will help you search for her," Nimika said assuredly.

"Are you sure?"

"Yes...stay here for a moment, please."

Nimaka floated slightly upwards, hovering only a few inches off the ground. She smoothly drifted away, as if on a puffy white cloud. The butterflies fluttered away with her.

Galax blinked his eyes, and stood anxiously, awaiting her return.

It wasn't long before Nimika reappeared. "She is ready to see you now," said the fae, and then disappeared again, deep into the forest.

Galax waited for Fortress, expecting a grand entrance. Several minutes had passed before he began to grow impatient.

Suddenly, he heard a loud noise coming from right in front of him. The ground shook slightly, and a mound of land shifted upwards—until a shapely woman emerged from the grass, dirt, and flowers that were breaking off into little chunks, and slipping from her head and shoulders. Her face turned a shade of green, and from her head sprouted long stems of whimsical vines that covered her body like a garment.

"I am Fortress, and you must be Galax," she said.

"Yes, I came here on an urgent mission," Galax replied. "With your help, I must retrieve the Keys of Fate."

"I already know of your mission, Galax. You needn't worry. I will help you."

"How did you—?"

"I have seen and heard the cries of the land. Amunet is weeping, and she asks me to heal and restore her body."

"Then you know what I have to do?"

Fortress walked around him, looking him over. She felt his memories, and watched as Elazar was enclosed in the sphere by Madicon.

"Elazar cannot help us, but he trusts you," she said thoughtfully. "And I trust him."

She was quiet again, pulling more of his memories. Galax eyed her surprisingly.

"Your friend, she needs our help," Fortress stated suddenly.

"Yes, she was taken by a crazy ghost."

"Have you solved the riddle?" she inquired.

"No, not yet, but I am working on it."

"Good. Let us go and save your friend. Then we will use the map to find the first key."

"I'm right behind you," Galax returned, as he followed her lead.

Fortress moved swiftly through the forest of Northford. She transferred with her surroundings, as if it was a part of her. There was no mistaking that she was the kind of fae that could manipulate particles of nature. That is why he needed her more than anything, if he was to retrieve the precious *keys* that were hidden within every crevice of Amunet's macrocosm.

Chapter Ten
Solving The Mystery

AT the foot of the hills, in the small town of Larksdale, Rimi McCracken stood in the doorway of
an abandoned house. He was carrying the warrior
woman in his arms, and for the moment, she was
completely unconscious. Rimi took dawdling steps,
and carefully set her down on a frumpy, grubby old
couch. A menacing black spider crawled up the arm-
rest, and quickly disappeared over the side.

Two houses down, a young woman sat reading
by the fireplace. She sighed longingly, and stared out
the window, in the deadness of night. The rain had
just begun beating the ground, and a few lightning
bolts flickered in the half-light.

Rimi paced back and forth continuously, pausing a couple of times in deep thought and anticipation of what he was about to do. The waiting was excruciating, and he had to keep a constant watch over Justise, checking to see that she was still out cold.

Through a cracked window, he saw the Bloodwyn transform into a man, and immediately thereafter was a loud knock at the door.

"Are you ready?" the hooded man asked, as he walked into the front room. "Are you sure you're ready for your fiancé to see you like this?"

"Yes, I'm ready." Rimi nervously answered. "I'm just not sure if this transfer will work?"

"Oh, it will work. Trust me."

"But why should I? Why are you so eager to help me?"

The man was quiet. He removed the hood from his head, and revealed his sullen face and shadowy eyes—eyes that widened with a coldness that chilled the damp air. "I have a score to settle," the man replied.

Rimi gazed bewilderingly at the man, remembering how he had come to him the night before, offering him a chance to reveal himself to his beloved fiancé. The man had seemed mad that night, but he had never questioned him, until now.

"What score do you have to settle with this woman?"

"She killed someone I loved," he resentfully remarked.

The man's anger overtook him, and he began to transform back into the vile thing that he was. Rimi watched in horror as the thick smoke oozing from the Bloodwyn's mouth, filled the area around him. In the turbid mists he could see Justise stabbing a knife into the back of a much thinner Bloodwyn, who was on the verge of attacking a man that was lying on the ground. Rimi recognized him as the one Justise had been traveling with.

In the background, just beyond the trees, Rimi could see that the Bloodwyn standing before him, had been at the scene. The Bloodwyn cleared the air by spewing a cool breeze, and then spoke evenly, "So you see. I am avenging the death of my lover. I will take the mystical sight that Justise used to find Galax, and give it to your fiancé. And one day, Justise will be helpless to see what is coming."

"So this is personal?" Rimi asked, not expecting a reply.

"Come now, we haven't much time," the Bloodwyn beckoned.

Fortress led Galax to the entrance of a cave, just outside the hidden realm of Northford. Galax stood at the mouth of it, nearly drained of energy. The journey was taking its toll on him, and he wished he was back at home in the castle, reading a study book, or writing a new enchantment for Elazar's approval.

In the back of his mind, he was concentrating on the mystery that Elazar had told him when he gave him the pyramid. He knew the time was approaching when he would have to solve the riddle, and he had not yet had a chance to come up with the right answer.

Fortress pulled at her hair, which was now forming a miniature tree patch near the tips of the strands. Tiny little branches sprang up, replacing the vines and leaves that had previously been there. The sun was settling in the west now, and as the darkness fell, a chilly wind caused Galax's nostril to sting.

"Where are we going?" Galax asked, rubbing the left side of his nose. "How much farther?"

"This is a shortcut, Galax. It's just right through this cave."

"Where are we going?" he asked. "Where did he take her?"

"If my senses are correct, he took her to his past, to where he used to live," Fortress stated.

"What?"

"He's after her abilities. I sensed that he is very much aware of her gift of sight."

"How did you know about that?"

"I know many things, and I can feel the emotions of this ghost, Galax. His name is Rimi McCracken. I have seen him roaming these woods, ever since the day he died. Your friend, Justise is just the person he's been looking for. I have reason to believe that he plans to transfer her powers to his fiancé Muriel."

"...but why? Why would he want to do that?"

Galax had been following steadily behind Fortress, but now he was purposely trying to get ahead of her.

"He wants his fiancé to see and communicate with him, which is what he has been trying to do since that fateful night. It's the only thing keeping him from crossing over into the netherworld."

"Well, is there anything else that can be done?" Galax asked. "Instead of taking Justise's powers, there has to be an alternative."

"There's only one," said Fortress. "If you get there first, you could give her the gift of sight."

A stream of twinkling lights, like a cluster of fireflies came into view, circling busily around Fortress' head, resting in the small tree patch that grew there. Galax could hear a faint sound, as if a tiny voice was trying to speak to him.

"The *Silent Wispers* are here to help you," Fortress earnestly said. "Follow their lights, teleport with them, and you should be there in minutes. I'll be right behind you."

"I already have a plan," Galax explained confidently. "So I'll see you when you get there."

Galax followed through time and space with

the *Silent Wispers* towards the town of Larksdale. It was raining fiercely there, and he was getting soaked from top to bottom. Reaching under his shirt, he pulled out the vial of *Labrygillius* "goo", and with a swift wave of his hand, he manifested a bottle of wine, wrapped in a blue ribbon. The *Silent Wispers* led him into the town square, and down a dark road. Galax's heart was racing wildly, as he pounded on the metal doorpost.

The pale young lady who answered, gazed upon him in curiosity. "Can I help you?" she politely asked.

"Yes, I'm here on behalf of Rimi McCracken," he said. "May I come in?"

Although she was hesitant, Muriel Larraine welcomed Galax into her home.

Rimi eye-balled the Bloodwyn, as he began the extraction of Justise's seeing power. He had his reservations that it would even work, but he was hopeful that he would soon be able to tell Muriel that he loved her, and wished that he had not died at sea. Muriel had no idea what had actually happened to Rimi. All she knew was that after their engagement, he had left for travel overseas, and never returned. Her heart was broken, to say the least, but she never stopped hoping that he would one day return. Although it had been several long years, Muriel was still in love, and determined to wait breathlessly for him.

The Bloodwyn released a small filament of mist from his eyes that swirled around Justise's body, eventually coasting into her nostrils and ear-holes. This awakened her, and she immediately choked on the mist, as her eyes became darkened and smoky.

"RIMI! RIMI, are you there?" A soft voice came from behind the walls of the weathered house.

Rimi looked up, startled, recognizing Muriel's sweet voice.

"Muriel?" he called.

Muriel walked through the walls, and stood in front of them, a ghostly figure. Rimi and the Bloodwyn were both astonished to see her in spirit form.

"Rimi, I have left my body to find you. I know what you're doing. It is wrong. You must come with me, now."

"Hold it right there, you're not going anywhere!" the Bloodwyn shouted.

"Come Rimi...hurry!" Muriel beckoned.

Rimi stared up into the chilling eyes of the Bloodwyn, as he released Justise from his long, blood-curdling fingers. The feathery fiend loomed over him like a strange unholy creature.

Just then, the abandoned house began to shake furiously, as if a tornado was tearing at its walls. In the middle of the commotion, Muriel reached out and grabbed Rimi's hand, leading him quickly into the forest, floating eerily out of sight.

Galax watched Rimi and Muriel disappear into the night, before preparing to teleport. Fortress had already begun generating a tornado, and so he knew he had to act fast. The Bloodwyn was infuriated by Rimi's defiance, and had turned again on Justise, who was too weak to fight back.

With the speed of light, Galax was in and out of the house in seconds, teleporting himself in just long enough to grab Justise, as Fortress used the wind to collapse the house upon the Bloodwyn.

In the forest of Rippingale, Justise, Fortress and Galax made their way through the tall brush, and found a place to sit down and rest. The heavy rains were now trickling, leaving a light misty steam in the air.

"Thank you, Galax, for coming to liberate me," Justise said. "You didn't have to do that. Now, I owe you one."

"No, now we're even, remember?"

"Right," Justise replied. "You must be Fortress. It is an honor to meet you," she said.

"I am," said Fortress, "and the honor is also mine." She had transformed her attire into a most agreeable outfit, which was a long green and white gown, after which her hair fell smoothly into lengthy tresses of russet curls.

"Do you have any idea where we're headed?" Fortress asked Galax.

"Not really. I need to solve the riddle to the pyramid map, and then I will know where we should go first."

"No, you need to eat first. I can sense your energy draining," Fortress demanded.

"Alright then, it won't take me long to get refreshed, and then we'll get going," Galax said.

"I'm starving..." Justise put in.

Galax figured that this would be the best place to mull over the riddle. He was really beginning to miss the comforts of home. Standing back, he took a few minutes to contemplate.

"Justise, I don't normally do this, but *Umfeatai delecticus!*" As he said these words, a round table of roasted chicken, fruits and vegetables appeared, adorned with fresh flowers and three goblets of delicious cold drinks.

"Let us enjoy this feast. I know you are hungry, and so am I."

"Thank you, Galax!" Justise answered. "I shall eat until I'm content."

She sat down on a chair that was tucked underneath, and proceeded to grind her teeth into a tender chicken leg.

"Pass the grapes please."

As she and Galax ate heartily, Fortress disappeared into the obscure shade of the forest trees. A moment later, she was standing on the edge of a small valley, staring out over the vast hills that could be seen for miles out. The *Silent Wispers* had accompanied her, as they were always near, fluttering enthusiastically around her head like glimmers of sunshine, whispering clandestinely in her ears. She spoke to them for several long minutes, in an ancient language of the fae.

Her long hair rose softly up her back, as she morphed the curls into tree branches and leaves again. The moon of Duldron hung in the sky, brightly lit, and fully visible. It could be seen even from a great distance, as though it was traveling toward Amunet, getting closer and closer to the planet. Fortress heard the *Silent Wispers* tell her that something was wrong with nature, and that Duldron was moving too closely to the atmosphere.

"What is it?" Galax came out of the woods, searching her eyes for a clue as to why she was so deep in thought.

"The moon...it draws too near," she said, turning to face him. "It is not a good sign."

"What do you suppose is happening?" asked Galax.

"Amunet is in great danger."

Suddenly, the *Silent Wispers* trailed away from Fortress and disappeared towards the moonlight.

Galax reached into the velvet pouch and pulled out the pyramid. He had a curious look on his face, as if he was troubled. Fortress nearly read his mind. She gestured for the pyramid, and asked him if he had a way of unlocking it.

"Well, Elazar said I should solve this riddle, and I haven't figured it out, yet.

"What is the riddle, and I'll try and help you," said Fortress.

"The key to the truth is like a mystery in a prism. The answer eludes you. When twilight comes, the dawn follows." Galax muttered. "What is that suppose to mean?"

"I'm not quite sure..."

"Well, I've pretty much decided that the first part of it has to do with the cubes and keys of fate. But the second part, I have no idea."

"What if it were referring to a time period? Twilight is around the middle of the night, and dawn is right before sunrise. Perhaps the map can only be seen during those hours."

"If you're right, then that is just a condition of the circumstances. There must be a way to actually trigger its activation."

"When twilight comes...the dawn—" Fortress turned the pyramid over a few times in her hand.

Galax's mind was racing with activity. "What about a state of mind?"

"What do you mean?" asked Fortress.

"Before you are enlightened, you must be in the dark, you know, confused."

"Yes, but how does that apply to the mystery and the keys of fate?"

"The answer is inside of me..."

"I think I understand," Fortress said. "The mysteries of the universe, the truth, do lie within the spirit. To activate the map, you must meditate to a higher state of being. You need to become more self-aware."

"I'm not sure what you're saying," Galax stated. "Can you be a little bit clearer?"

"I've not seen this type of metal before. Nor have

I seen this advanced mechanics on our planet. I assume that this device is not from our world, which means, you cannot activate it with a physical key. Use your mind Galax, and connect with it. I think it is saying that *you hold the key*."

Fortress handed Galax the pyramid, and stood back, giving him some breathing room. Galax concentrated on the device, and for a long moment, nothing happened. Then, he remembered something. He saw flashes of the parchment from Elazar's secret compartment; the scrolls in which were written instructions for *Light Making*.

With this thought, Galax strolled away from Fortress, and sat down on a large boulder to concentrate. He was now facing the valley, overlooking the enormous moon of Duldron. In his mind, he envisioned himself inside of the pyramid, and then inside a sphere, and then inside of a cube. Creating an atmosphere of stars on the walls of the cube, he then focused his meditation on the sphere, as the planet of Amunet appeared as a transparent hologram.

Staring at the holographic map, which was now visible to Fortress, she said, "I knew you could do it!"

"Do what?" Justise asked, as she strode up beside them, gawking impressively at the surrounding depiction. "Whoa...what's going on here?"

"Galax has just unraveled the map of the planet, and the location of the *Keys of Fate*."

The planet's projection began to expand, and Galax noticed a large crack forming, like a quake, rippling through the planet. The hologram was highlighting one of the missing keys in blue, while showing the fault of the quake in red.

"Look, something is wrong here," Galax said, pointing to the key.

"We have to get moving, first thing in the morning," Fortress said. "I know exactly where the key is, and it looks like the inhabitants will be in big trouble if we don't get there quickly. We'll travel faster if we're rested."

"It's the work of the Ember Trolls. I knew this was coming. See Galax, I told you our missions are connected," Justise exclaimed.

Suddenly, Justise had a vision. She could see the extinction of the winged people, the Shikoba, and only one remained.

"Yes, Justise. I guess so," said Galax.

Fortress was worried about the disturbances in nature more than anyone. She knew that from the looks of it, Amunet was undergoing a major geological transformation. To her, the Ember Trolls held in their power, a device so destructive, they could wipe out the very existence of life on Amunet.

Chapter Eleven
The Inseparable Two

THE heat rose up like a blazing inferno, steam burning the thick skins of the Shikoba, a tribe of winged people. As the earth opened wider around their land, a rare forest of enormously tall redwood trees, fire from a disturbed phoenix ignited, racing through their nesting houses.

One brave wolf, Ulrike, stayed behind, after his pack had ran out of the forest at first sense of trouble. Ulrike would not leave his friend, Torin, the Archer.

Torin had heard Ulrike's warning before all the others, and was on his way to warn them, when he had caught sight of the giant Perceval, clinging to the edge of the terrain for dear life. Perceval was a lonely giant that had lived peacefully among the Shikoba for many years. Torin heard his cry and went to him, grabbing his arm, trying desperately to save him.

The Phoenix of fire was out of control. The gases from the ozone hole that had suddenly encircled their village had already killed most of his clan. A few Shikoba men that had tried flying over the deathly ring, had died from the steam, pulling them down into the smothering pit of infinite depth below.

Torin held on to Perceval's arm, sweating excessively, and begging him not to let go. There was only a split second chance that he would be able to pull his hefty body to safety, and he did not know if he would have the strength to do so.

Ulrike barked constantly, warning him of the time they had left to flee, but even with the thought of imminent death, still he would not leave his friend.

From the sky, a fireball crashed a few feet in front of Ulrike, burning a small bush of leaves. It had descended from the wings of the phoenix of fire, as she had passed over them, screeching madly in utter shock and panic.

It wasn't her fault that she could not control her flames. The flames were a result of her emotions, which were surging with fear and alarm. She had her own worries. Her nest was just a few miles in the redwood forest. There was an egg there that needed to be protected, but there was no one left to retrieve it.

Fortress was swift to action. She had arrived with

the wind, assessing the damage from above, and immediately called the phoenix of fire to the safer side of the terrain to calm her.

"The devastation is too great for me alone to handle, Galax," Fortress said. "I'll have to call for help."

"Well, what can we do to assist you?" Galax asked, looking about in frustration. He knew his own enchantments would be of no use here, but he still had to retrieve the *Key of Fate*, which according to the map, was about a mile or so inland, in a darkened cave.

"Rescue the Shikoba, if any remain, and I will attempt to control this catastrophe. You can ride on the phoenix, once she is consoled. Her aura will protect you from the heat and the fire."

The large phoenix landed with a loud thud, wings stretched out wide and fearsome. Galax and Justise watched in awe as Fortress began to light into flames, touching the phoenix on the head, soothing her, conversing telepathically with her, until both their flames began to settle.

"Galax, I will collect the phoenix tears for you, and you must sprinkle them on her nest in the cave. That is where the key of fate is hidden, and only her phoenix tears will allow you to put out her flames. All the phoenix asks is that you rescue her egg, and bring it back safely."

"I will," Galax replied, as he manifested a potion bottle, and handed it to Fortress.

The tears of the phoenix fell gradually from her eyes. Sparkling like diamonds, they were collected in the bottle until it was filled. After handing it back to Galax, Fortress disappeared again into the airstream.

Galax and Justise mounted the phoenix, and rode off into the smothering clouds of smoke and steam. As they crossed the ring, Justise noticed the giant Perceval, and the winged Shikoba man at the edge of the forest. Torin was losing his grip, and even though he was in tremendous pain, he continued to hold the giant by the arm.

"LET ME GO!" Perceval shrieked, eyes bulging in anticipation and fear.

"NO...*hold on!*" Torin yelled; sweat dripping profusely from his forehead. "I won't let you go."

"You have to," Perceval pleaded.

Perceval was slipping, and he was afraid that he would pull Torin down with him.

"*Please—*" Perceval begged, his brows furrowing deeply in concern.

Although Torin would not release him until the very last moment, Perceval slipped away into the ozone hole, and disappeared out of sight.

Ulrike was quick, grabbing Torin's shirt, and pulling him away from the edge of danger.

The phoenix landed near Torin, who lay down

on the ground, smeared in ash, badly burned and dying. He was the last of his clan, as all the rest had perished in the disaster.

Galax looked up, "What's that?" he said, pointing to a speckle in the sky that was rapidly moving towards them.

"I guess Fortress found the help she was looking for," Justise said.

A shrill, piercing noise caught their attention, as three phoenixes appeared, flying together towards the redwood forest. A hypnotic blue phoenix, dripping of water, flew swiftly to and fro, sprinkling her droplets on the burning treetops and vegetation that grew abundantly in the woodland.

The second phoenix was white, and she encircled the redwoods continuously, releasing an icy breeze into the air, clearing away the steam. The cloudiness receded, and the debris from the Shikoba's nesting houses, became visible through the smog.

The third phoenix was black, and she was a great help to Fortress. She dropped soil, filling in the heat pockets, as the nature fae used her elemental power over the land, to push the two terrains back together again. It was a monumental task, and as Fortress diligently altered the planet's surface, Galax checked to see if the Shikoba man was still breathing.

"He's alive!" he shouted, as Justise dismounted the fire phoenix, and made her way over to them.

"Can you hear me?" Galax asked. "What is your name?"

"Torrr....rin," he groaned, opening his eyes briefly, and then closing them again.

Relieved, Ulrike rushed to his side to eagerly lick his face. He was glad to see that Torin had awakened, and would possibly live long enough to be rescued.

"You were very brave, Torin," Justise said. "We will take care of you. Don't worry. I won't leave you." She grabbed his hand, holding it tightly. She was intrigued with the winged man, and had resolved to keep him from dying.

"I have to go," Galax said to Justise. "I have to go and get the key."

"Is there any magic that you can do to save him?" Justise asked.

Galax looked down at Torin, who had drifted into a deep sleep. "No, he's too far gone. There's nothing I can do for him."

"Is there anything that can be done?" Justise asked again.

"Wait for Fortress, as she'll know how to save him," said Galax. "I won't take long. I promised the phoenix that I'd retrieve her egg, so I'll be back in a while."

"Alright Galax, but you be careful."

"I will," Galax said, mounting the phoenix again. The phoenix flew Galax to the cave where her nest was located. She had calmed down quite a bit, and was determined to move her egg somewhere safe from the disaster happening all over again. When they arrived, Galax dismounted, and spoke softly to the phoenix before he went in.

"I'll only be a short time and I promise to bring you your egg," he assured her. She let one huge teardrop fall from her right eye, and the moment it hit the ground, a spiky ice crystal was formed. Galax, guessing it might come in handy, picked it up and headed into the blackness.

Inside, the cave was crawling with many luminous ember spiders, scampering away from his feet as he passed. He was not afraid of them, but he knew and had read about their venomous bite. Just one puncture would cause your veins to be scorched with convulsive heat, and your body would explode within minutes thereafter.

A rather fearsome spider crawled along the ceiling, following his path. The glow from his markings alerted Galax, and he stood completely still, anticipating what the spider was up to. Before Galax could move, it pounced on his arm, attempting to injure him.

Galax was ready. With a flick of his hand, he shoved it off. The spider went flying into the shadows before him, but that didn't stop it. It started screeching and charged for him, aiming to take a big bite out of his face. Without much thought, Galax pulled out the ice crystal, and stabbed the spider in the chest. The frost from the sparkler was powerful magic, sending the arachnid into a screaming rage of kicking legs, until it died unwillingly in agony.

A little bit of light flickered from deep within the cave. As he approached it, he felt the sweltering heat from the circle of eternal flames that engulfed an immense nest of ashes. Taking out the elixir of phoenix tears, he drank a swig, and then began to sprinkle drops on the fiery blaze. As the fire began to die down, he approached the nest where the huge egg was laying, and noticed the shiny key lying beneath it.

The key was too hot to handle, but the elixir had allowed him to touch it without getting burned. Carefully, he grabbed the egg, and tucked it under his arm. Then he headed quickly back out of the cave.

The phoenix took him back to Justise and Torin. When he arrived, he saw Fortress coming out of the forest, and following her were the other three phoenixes.

"How is he?" Fortress asked.

"He's still alive, but I don't know how much longer he will live. His breathing is getting more unstable. Is there anything you can do?" Justise asked.

"Yes, if we hurry, we can take him to the goddess of Destiny. She is a special being. She will know how to save his life," Fortress replied.

"I can teleport him," Galax stated. "It would take less time."

"I'm afraid that's impossible, Galax. The goddess lives deep in the forest of Northford. There is no way to teleport past the enchantments. You'll have to fly. The phoenixes will take you. They know how to get there."

"What about you?" asked Galax. "Aren't you coming with us?"

"I'll be there as soon as I can. First, I must carry the egg to a safe haven, where the fire phoenix can build a new nest."

Galax carefully handed her the iridescent egg,

which he had been holding in his arms.

"It won't take long," she stated.

"What do I do when I get to the village? Where do I go?" asked Galax.

"Look for my sister, Queen Illustra. She will help you. I have already sent her a message through the *Silent Wispers*, so she will be expecting you."

Fortress spoke softly to each phoenix as it stepped forward. The first of the phoenixes to approach them had blue feathers. Galax levitated Torin, gently placing him comfortably on the phoenix's back.

The black and the white phoenixes approached next, and Galax and Justise quickly mounted them. Ulrike barked at Galax reproachfully.

"Don't worry, my friend...I haven't forgotten you," Galax said, grinning down at him. The white phoenix he had mounted began to gently hover off the ground. His giant wings stretched impressively outward, as he powered up his strength to take flight. With a swift jerk, he picked up Ulrike in his claws, and carried them both into the evening sky, headed towards the north.

Turning to look around, Galax saw Justise and Torin just a little ways behind him. He had used an enchantment to strap Torin to the phoenix to prevent him from falling off during their passage.

The wind was fierce, but the sun was temper-

ate, and felt invitingly therapeutic. Galax was relieved that he had retrieved one of the *Keys of Fate*.
He wondered what he should do with it. His satchel
contained only one cube. Even without instruction,
he knew he would have to use it, but he was unsure
how to set things right. He wished he could talk to
Elazar. Even a word of advice would help put his
mind at ease.

There was so much that had to be done, and he
felt like the task was too much to handle. What if I
am unable to stop the next catastrophe? He was sure
there would be another one soon. Once he was in
Northford, and the Shikoba was healed, he would
have to look at the map again. There was no telling
what the Ember Trolls were planning to do next.

In the distance, Galax saw Fortress and the fire
phoenix soaring towards the west. Fortress' likeness
was indistinct, and he guessed she was using the
force of the wind as her ride. What a wonderful way
to fly, he thought.

Chapter Twelve
The Alchemy of Life and Death

THE phoenixes touched down on a high cliff, overlooking the fae village. The view was captivating, as the weather was always perfect in the land of the fae. However, of their group, only Galax could see the village below, as it was quietly nestled behind numerous protective spells and charms. Illustra was already waiting, ready to welcome them to Northford. She was there to ensure that they were safely escorted past the enchantments.

Galax laid Torin on the crystal slab that Illustra provided. It floated just two feet above the ground, and glided smoothly beside her, as she led them into the village.

Not long after they had entered the hidden vale,

Illustra stopped short, and spoke to Galax. "Silvica will see that you reach the goddess of Destiny," she stated, pointing just a few feet away, between two large trees. Silvica was an unusual sight to behold. She had long black straight hair, and wore a blue, white, and black dress that matched the colors of several small birds that were perched on her shoulders. Three little ones flew down from the treetops, following a ray of sunlight, and circled her head before resting on her outstretched arms. She smiled warmly, as Galax's entourage approached her.

"I will see to them," she said softly to Ilustra.

Illustra nodded to her appreciatively, and said a brief goodbye, before drifting serenely towards the outlying palace, as if she had many things to attend to.

"This way...it isn't that far," Silvica gestured. She seemed to have attached her mind to the crystal slab, because it moved beside her now, as they walked hurriedly through the forest.

They passed a fae with wavy teal hair, who stood in a shimmering sunbeam, as a multitude of bouncing, pastel-tinted crickets leaped prettily about, some whose wings and antennas were harmoniously illuminated. The crickets had exceptionally long eyelashes, and large eyes that were sweetly mesmerizing. The fae was listening attentively to the melodious chirping song of a cricket that was balancing on the edge of a sizable leaf. She looked up, and bowed graciously to Silvica as they passed.

"That was Azura," Silvica announced. "She says hello, and wishes you many blessings on your journey."

"Will you thank her for me?" Galax asked, as he nodded appreciatively to Azura.

"Oh, she already knows."

The sun was going down in the west, sinking slowly into a tranquil sleep. They were approaching a dazzling pond filled with many aquatic plants, including hundreds of pink water lilies. At the front of the stone bridge that crossed the pond, sat two large statue heads, showering a stream of water noisily from their mouths. Silvica led them over, heading towards an enchanted door that was nestled in a wall of rose bushes.

Stunned to see two roses coming to life, Galax moved closer, watching Silvica as she raised her hand up to them. One of the roses entwined itself around her thumb, pricking it, producing a pinch of silver colored blood. Immediately the rose transmuted into metal, as the blood from Silvica raced down the stem, and altered the whole bush. In the moments that followed, Galax curiously studied the roses, as they actively turned a number of metallic engravings and shifted gears on the door, unlocking it.

The other side of the hideaway seemed al-

most like a different world all-together. There were many types of flowers blooming everywhere. Nature seemed to have created a private nook, surrounded by branches, and protected from the rest of the world. A brilliant and sparkling light shined down from some unknown hole in the top of the secret garden. Silvica led them over to a colossal wall, and removed some of the vines that were crawling up the cracks.

"This place looks deserted," Justise said, glancing around and behind her for signs of life.

"Here, we have to activate the star vehicle, and call the goddess," said Silvica.

"Well, how do we do that?" Galax questioned, staring up at the carvings in the ancient stone. It was a puzzle to him.

"There are six words that represent the alchemy of life and death. They must be said consecutively, and when all the lights have lit up along the sides of this crystal flower in the center, the goddess will leave the higher realms, and return to us."

On one side of the crystal was the inscription, *"Alchemy of Life,"* while on the other side was written, *"Alchemy of Death."*

"I hope you know what the code words are, because I have no idea," said Galax.

"Yes, I do," said Silvica. "Stand back, while I activate the crystal."

Galax and Justise stepped sideways a few feet, and watched Silvica take a long, meditative breath. For several minutes she looked directly at the first orb disk in the wall.

"Innocence," said Silvica, as she waited for the orb disk to reflect light. At first, all was quiet, but then after a brief moment, the disk filled with a heavenly, starry light, and then swirled a golden mist that moved in a circular motion.

"...Love...Peace," said Silvica, and the other two disks under the words, *"Alchemy of Life,"* were also triggered.

Galax and Justise exchanged thankful looks at each other. Torin was barely breathing now, and Ulrike sat down on the ground, patient and alert.

"...*Suffering...Wisdom...Change*," said Silvica, as the other three disks lit up under the inscription, "*Alchemy of Death.*"

Instantly the crystal in the center of the orb disks activated, and a blast of luminous light beamed outwards. The light was blinding, and so each of them turned away for the duration of the flare.

When they had recovered from the brilliance, there stood a tiny being. She was a little over one foot tall, and held a most gracious expression on her face. Her eyes danced lovingly, and Galax felt her light-heartedness.

"Hello," she said. "I have been waiting for you."

"Hello flower goddess...will you heal this Shikoba, and bring him back to us," Silvica asked.

The tiny goddess floated over to Torin, still lying on the slab, and then preceded towards a huge mound of dirt, in the midst of the garden.

"Because he sacrificed his life to save the giant's, his breath will be revived," she stated. She took from her pouch, a small crystal seed, and planted it in the mound.

"Place the body of this Shikoba on the bed of thorns, and when the roses bloom, it will rejuvenate his blood," said the goddess.

Galax used his levitation powers to lift Torin over to the bed of thorns, which instantaneously grew out from the soil. The thorns became thicker and thicker, and eventually they twined their stems around Torin's body, and pricked him in several places.

Slowly the thorns receded from the vines, and roses began to bloom in their stead. For a while Galax paced around the bed, studying the effects of the roses, as they worked their magic. Torin's bruises healed, and his face became less darkened and frail. His heart beat loudly for a second, and then he took a gulping breath of air, and sat up bewildered. His wings flapped uncontrollably for several minutes until he became emotionally settled.

He thought he was in a strange place, that maybe he had died and awakened in the netherworld. It was Justise's soothing face that relaxed him. He remembered her sitting next to him, holding his hand, and saying that she would not let him die. He looked at her, deep in her eyes, with sincere adoration.

"What happened?" he cried.

"You have survived the catastrophe. But the people of your clan did not," answered Galax. "I'm sorry, Torin."

Ulrike howled ecstatically, and rushed gratefully to his side. "Calm down, old boy," said Torin, embracing the wolf. "I must have given you such a fright."

Justise swallowed hard. "I'm sorry that we could not save your people in time," she apologized. Torin's face fell. His horrific memories were slowly coming back. The sorrow swept over him like a tidal wave.

Justise reached out and put her arms around his shoulders, holding him for a while, as he wept. Her heart went out to him, and she felt empathy for his unbearable pain and grief.

Everyone was silent. Galax was now concerned about Fortress. He hoped she had already arrived in Northford. He wondered how she was faring, and if she'd found a safe place for the fire phoenix to nest her egg.

The tiny goddess spoke decisively, "I leave with you these precious gifts of silver. It is your destiny to help Galax on *his* quest to retrieve the *Keys of Fate*. Have peace in the deliverance of this task that is set before you." A silver bow and arrow appeared next to Torin. He picked them up, inspecting their superior craftsmanship.

"Thank you goddess," he said. "I will do my duty."

The goddess nodded assuredly, and within a split second, she had disappeared in a beam of light.

After an hour, Torin had completely re-energized, and was ready to travel. He and Justise had taken a strong liking to one other, expressing tenderness of touch, without saying much at all. Ulrike lingered reservedly by the garden's entrance for the Archer. He was anxious to see him take flight again. Flying was a sure sign to him that Torin had fully recovered.

"Silvica, I'm glad that he has made it through,"

Galax said, as they strode towards the bridge.

"Yes, I guess it was his destiny," she answered.

Galax grinned agreeably. "Well, I am still learning about destiny, and how it affects our plight."

"Destiny is part your will, and the will of the Creator. Together, it forms a tie that is unbreakable. Following your destiny, is like strengthening your bond to all living things. Each step you take towards fulfillment gets you closer to perfection, which is the purpose of destiny."

"I see...so my destiny is to retrieve the *Keys of Fate*, and the closer I get to completing it, the more perfected my spirit will become?"

"Yes, you understand the principle."

"Perfection is also becoming a co-creator, a *Light Maker*, and existing in the peace that extends the Creator's love to all things. It is your fate, because you were especially chosen to not only bring back the *Keys*, but to use them to restore this planet to its utopian state."

"You are very wise," Galax remarked.

When they had reached the nexus of the forest, Torin stretched out his wings, taking off rapidly towards the hazy night clouds. His heavy wings beat briskly against the wind with such force, that he was sure he was in better health now, than he had been in his whole life. *Something must have changed in me*, he thought.

Ulrike raced through the forest of Northford, following the soaring Shikoba, darting zealously between trees and bushes, and chasing his shadow when it fell close to the ground.

Fortress greeted them happily upon their entrance to the palace halls of Northford. She had prepared warmly lit rooms for them, and a grand meal was set out in the dining hall. Many of the fae were moving busily about, most attending to private matters pertaining to their appointments. Each greeted the guests as they passed, with loving thoughts that they could hear telepathically as they were escorted to their quarters.

Galax woke up continuously, not able to sleep in peace, and got out of bed. Deep in the night, as the wind blew a gentle breeze through the gardens, Galax walked the grounds—lit by various fluttering *Silent Wispers*—and contemplated the circumstances in front of him. He had the key in his pocket, and he kept touching it lightly, checking to see that it was still in his care. He missed Elazar, his study, and his daily routines. It seemed like ages ago since he'd left the castle, and he knew that nothing in his life would ever be the same again.

He turned abruptly towards a shifting silhouette. He could hear scratching, and the sounds of stirring branches. He was a little frightened, but then he saw what was veiled in the folds of the shade.

"Oh, it is you," he said to Fortress, as he realized she was leaning against the trunk of a slender tree, blending in flawlessly with the bark. "I didn't mean to disturb you."

He turned to leave.

"It's alright. I was just listening to Amunet, as she spoke to me," Fortress replied. "She is concerned for her children, the inhabitants of the east."

"Amunet is right," said Galax, turning around to face her. "I couldn't sleep. I saw something in my dreams that bothered me."

"What is it? Have you checked the map?"

"Yes, I have. Tomorrow we head towards the Genesis Sea. The key is underwater, and a calamitous disaster is also predicted."

"The Ember Trolls again?"

"I'm afraid so. It gets worst. The map has shown me terrible things are occurring on the ocean's floor. I saw a tsunami building up that could wipe out the entire region."

Fortress sighed. "Something must be done about those Trolls. Where are the *Wizards of the Kingdoms*? What are they doing about this? This eco-machine is getting out of hand."

"I spoke to Justise, and she has asked me to join forces with Prince Nolan of Osnath."

"Well...what have you decided?"

"Nothing yet... I just don't know if I should get involved. I don't think I can help him. I'm not as powerful as Madicon. I wish Elazar was around to guide me."

"If Elazar were here, what do you think he would tell you to do?"

Galax's brow furrowed lightly, as he imagined himself staring into Elazar's thoughtful eyes. "He would probably not be too impressed with me right about now. I'm moving at a snail's pace. I should have retrieved more keys, and—"

"You are wrong. He would be quite proud," interrupted Fortress. "I know him."

Galax pulled the ancient key from his pocket, and showed it to Fortress.

"What would he tell me to do with this key?"

"I cannot advise you on that one. Perhaps you should think about it a little longer. Right now, you've only got one key, and I recommend that you use it wisely."

"I know, but am I supposed to wait, and return them all to him. I'm not sure if I'm the right one for this task. It is so confusing to me."

"If Elazar believed in you, then you're the right one for this task. You may not believe me when I say this, but I'm sure he has trained you for this very moment. Trust in your abilities. You will do well, if you just have a little more faith. There is a reason to this madness. It may not make sense to you now, but one day, it will."

"Well... maybe you're right. I just wish I could talk to Elazar. I wish I could turn back, and rescue him."

"Perhaps there is a way—" Fortress commented, staring down at the key.

Galax thought for a moment, and then smiled.

"I will give this more consideration, but we must get to Genesis first," he affirmed. "Depending on what we find there, we might truly need this fateful key."

"Then there we will go...first thing in the morning," she agreed. "Until then, try and get some sleep."

Chapter Thirteen
A Royal Aide

AT first light, Galax rose early, and made his way into the great hall of the palace. He had not slept more than a wink the night before. Fortress was speaking quietly to her sister, the queen of Northford, about the long task ahead. Illustra glanced graciously at Galax, as soon as she saw him saunter in.

"Come here Galax, I have something for you," she insisted. "I have heard that you are having trouble contacting Elazar. I have seen through my crystal that he is trapped inside a sphere of magical power. I cannot unleash him from this curse, but I can offer you another way of reaching him."

Galax's eyes brightened at the thought of receiving clear instructions from Elazar again.

"What must I do in order to see him?"

Illustra motioned to one of the fae, which brought her a jeweled case. "The blade on this dagger is made of a unique gemstone, and it is strong enough to cut through the fabric of reality. It is called the *Blade of Ismene*. Use it, and it will temporarily bring Elazar within your reach. But remember, he will only appear to be in your presence. The enchantment on his body will not be broken. Also, once you use it, you must let it's cosmic energy recharge before using it again."

"I understand. Thank you, Illustra. This gift will be very helpful to me," Galax answered, holding the dagger carefully, and studying the blade that was so shear, it did not appear to be there at all. It seemed as if he was holding nothing, but a crack in reality—it was however, a true window into the broken shards of the space-time continuum. He placed it carefully in a soft cloth, and hid it under his garment for safe keeping.

When he and Fortress were alone on the balcony overlooking the river of Athanasia, he spoke confidently to her. "I should go privately, and speak to Elazar before we leave. There is so much I need to ask him about what I should do with this key," he said.

"Remember that the blade must be recharged after every use. You don't know how long it will take. Perhaps you should wait until a time that is more challenging. You might need him then."

"You are wise, Fortress," Galax replied. "I will hold off until we have reached the next location on the map. I'll want to know what he requires of me, once I have retrieved the second key."

"I'm glad you agree. I'm told that everyone is ready to go, and I'm also prepared for the dangerous expedition ahead. Did you get any sleep?"

"Not really, but I drank an elixir that I created this morning. It will help me keep my energy up, so I'll be fine."

"Good, you'll need your energy, where we're going," she admitted.

Galax sought out his companions. They had been killing time outside the palace in the lush gardens. Justise was practicing throwing her two daggers at a tree. She was startled, when she saw her hawk, Nellie, flying down to meet her.

"Nellie, looks like you have a message for me?" She took the note that was tied to the bird's leg and read:

Dear Ms. Justise,

I have attempted several times to locate Mortighan Remus Shalshank to no avail. He did come to visit the shop earlier, but I have not seen him at the festival for several days now. It has been reported, that he may have returned to his home town of Penne Luxford. I will send word to him there that you are looking for him.

Warm Regards,

Dacey De Boteler

Dacey De Boteler,
Magic Seeds and Beans

"Alright, Nellie...you've been a good girl," Justise whispered, stroking her feathery back. "I don't think Mortighan is in Penne Luxford, though. I would have felt it if he were there. Will you fly out again, and continue your search?"

Nellie screeched a sharp reply, and then flew off towards the bright morning sun.

Galax and Fortress entered the garden.

"Good morning, Justise...did you sleep well?" Fortress asked.

"Yes, very well...actually."

"That is good, because we have some serious miles to cover."

"We're going to the Genesis Sea," explained Galax, glancing upwards as Torin glided down around the area where their horses were feeding. Then he flew horizontally, circling the tree tops. This was his morning habit, allowing him plenty of fresh sunshine, and exercise for his wings.

"The Genesis Sea—" Justise repeated. "Well, this should be interesting. By the way, I have already filled Torin in on all the details, and he is anxious to help you on your quest."

"Is everyone ready then?" Galax asked.

"We're all yours...you just lead the way and we'll follow you." Ulrike yelped excitedly in eagerness to begin what he believed was an adventure.

"Let's get going, then...the tribes of Genesis need our help," Galax requested, as he saddled up Sugar Cane, who had been found wandering in the outlying forest, and brought to the palace.

He knew that the road to the Genesis Sea would carry them into uncharted territory, but he was sure that with Fortress at his side, nothing could prevent them from reaching their destination.

The day grew hot and muggy, and the sun beat down on their backs as they drove their horses onward. They stopped often to drink fresh water from nearby lakes and streams. Fortress led the way, as they wandered over large rocks and down steep mountains. They were traveling towards a long stretch of patchy landscape, where there was little shade for them to rest under. Torin and Ulrike were always a mile ahead of them, drifting like specks of dust near the horizon.

Movement was always eastward, to the ancient lands—the birthplace of magic and all that was mystical in the world of Amunet. Torin had agreed to keep watch from the clear blue sky. From time to time, he would bring them back information on what he had seen, and how much farther they were from towns, fishing ports, rivers, and lakes.

Around midday, Galax was growing restless. He thought that if he could get there a little faster, maybe the damage would not be so great. He feared for what they were likely to find. *What if the key is lost? What if I cannot retrieve it?*

Justise felt a strong jerk coming from her stomach, and she knew she was about to have another vision. She saw several Bloodwyns rising from the trees, attacking Torin, and dragging him into the darkness of the thick woods of Maia.

She gazed up, but could not see where he had gone. The woods of Maia were just three miles away from them. However, once they had entered the shrouded forest, it would be difficult to trace Torin, if he had been taken.

"What is it?" Galax questioned. He could tell that something was terribly wrong, by the frowned expression on Justise's face.

"It's Torin...he's in danger," she answered, speeding up her horse.

"Bloodwyns!" bellowed Fortress. "I can hear

them coming...we must hurry!"

They were all riding fast and hard now. Fortress had taken to wind, and was searching the clouds, looking for signs of Torin, and the approaching Bloodwyns.

They had not yet reached the umbrella of tall trees, when Ulrike came running out of the thicket. Torin was right behind him, flying low to the ground. He did not seem to perceive the uneasiness of his approaching comrades. He flew upwards, and stopped midair, noticing Justise was screaming at the top of her lungs, but he could not hear what she was saying.

"I can't hear you!" he yelled.

A moment later, he saw a silver dagger whizzing pass his left shoulder. Pumped with adrenaline, he turned to see behind him. The dagger hit a Bloodwyn in the chest. All he noticed was a dark mist rising from the shadows below.

There were many more Bloodwyns than Justise had perceived. Perhaps there were twenty of them, maybe even thirty. She had stopped counting. With swiftness, she dismounted her horse, and prepared for the impending attack.

Torin had already pulled out his sacred bow and arrow, given to him by the goddess of Destiny, and fired at the closest Bloodwyn in range. The arrow was unusually accurate, without him even trying. To make matters more extraordinary, the arrow immediately found its way back to his bow, ready to be fired out again.

Galax was now standing in the darkest haze he had ever been in. The thick fog of Bloodwyn feathers reached out like a smoky noose, grabbing at his throat. He moved rapidly, teleporting himself in and out of the mist, darting away from them, as they tried to seize him.

He built up a force field around his body, and then pulled out a long staff that slid out from a tubular case. Immediately, he began powering up a surge of electric shockwaves. Positioning himself defensively, he struck the Bloodwyns rhythmically with both ends of the staff, as they steadily encircled him. He caught a glimpse of Justise stabbing vigorously at many Bloodwyns, the moment they reached out for her. She had already killed more than three of them, and was working on a fourth, when he decided to send Fortress a telepathic message.

"Pull them back, away from us, and I will shield us off," he uttered, hitting a Bloodwyn with one end of his staff. The energy sent heavy shockwaves through the enemy's bird-like body, causing tremendous pain—before its heart stopped completely, and it trans-morphed into a human. "There are too many of them!" he yelled.

Fortress heard Galax's words very clearly. She began gathering a huge gust of wind, pulling the Bloodwyns towards her, and away from him, so he could form his protective barrier. As the Bloodwyns were tossing backwards in the air, Fortress directed storm clouds to come together in the vicinity.

The skies grew dim, as the wind blew forcefully. Thunder and lightning took over the atmosphere. Galax and the others watched as an incredibly large glob of water fell from the cloud above them, and smacked the top of the force shield. It made a deafening noise, as it slid down the side and hit the ground. *Thunk...*

A moment later, another glob fell, and then a few more. *Thunk...thunk...thunk...* Soon the rain was falling heavily, pouring down globs of water, splashing into mud ponds. A cluster of Bloodwyns were unexpectedly strickened, and once splattered, Fortress froze them solid, encasing them in ice. This caused huge chunks of plummeting hailstone to come crashing to the ground. The land shook continuously, as several of the ice blocks smacked into one another, causing dynamic impacts.

Quite a few Bloodwyns were ducking away from the mammoth raindrops, and knocking into the force shield, which was withstanding maximal pressure from the constant beating.

"Look, someone's coming!" yelled Torin. He was ascending near the top of the domed shield, where he could witness armored men on horses racing towards them.

"It's an army," Justise returned. "And they are carrying the flags of Osnath."

Galax moved closer so he could capture a peek at them. Another huge torrent of water hit the side of the shield, sliding down right in front of him. He had to wait several moments before he could see clearly.

"Yes, it is the prince. I wonder if they are coming to aide in our defense. It seems as they may just as well, pass us by."

Prince Nolan ordered his frontline to fire arrows at the Bloodwyns, while a second team of his men dismounted their horses, and fought with sharpened swords. Galax was encouraged, shutting off the shield, and allowing his companions to rejoin in combat.

Most of the Bloodwyns were fleeing, while the others fought boldly. Galax's main concern was protecting the key and the cube. He had brought only one cube with him, and he knew that the Bloodwyns were after it. With it, Madicon could change the fate of the battle again, and if he were to think of other destructive uses, the world of Amunet would truly be in peril.

Within a half hour, the Bloodwyns had been defeated. There were none left, except those encased in the blocks of ice that were scattered in the background. One at a time, Galax teleported the heavy chunks to the tops of the highest snow-capped mountains within range. There, they would stay frozen, until some other form of magic released them from their coolers.

When he returned, Justise and Fortress were sitting at a table eating dinner, and talking to Prince Nolan in the royal canvas that his men had set up at the edge of the forest of Maia.

Upon entering the tent, he was greeted respectfully. "I could use a wizard like you, Galax," Prince Nolan exclaimed. "You are very courageous to be taking on such a momentous task."

Galax looked over confusingly at Justise, who

was grinning back at him.

"You have told him?" he barked.

"I have told him that you mean to stop Madicon, and the evil Ember Trolls from destroying our planet."

"My father will be indebted to you for helping us," Prince Nolan replied, drinking a sip of wine. "It is an honor to aide you on your quest." He waved at a soldier, who immediately brought Galax a plate of food, and a goblet of wine.

Galax was starving, but he was also thinking about Elazar. Now would be a good time to contact him. Fortress said very little. She offered no comfort to him, nor did she advise him on what he should do next.

"I am on your side, my Lord," Galax said. "I am no Mage, like Madicon, King Hasad's counselor, but I know a way that he can be defeated. It is important that we help each other in this war."

"I agree, Galax. It is imperative that you and I stay connected. For the next few days, we will ride together. I offer you protection, and anything else you might require."

"Well, there is one thing," Galax admitted. "You must not surrender, under any circumstances."

"And why would I surrender?" the prince asked surprisingly.

"I know that your men are losing the battle as we

speak. I want you to wait for me, because I will use magic to help you gain advantage over them."

The prince was astounded by these words. Fortress and Justise were both eyeing Galax seriously, waiting to hear the rest of his plan.

"Go on, you have my full attention," said Prince Nolan.

"I will soon be releasing a power that will change the fate of the battle. It is your destiny to defeat King Hasad, and for Madicon to be outmaneuvered. If you fail, Amumet could be destroyed."

"I see...I will do my best to remain in the war. You have my word. I will not surrender, as you have requested," the prince promised.

"Good," said Galax.

"We should head out at early dawn," Prince Nolan said. "My cousin, Kagen, is waiting on our reinforcements. Is there anything you need? A few of my men, perhaps?"

"No...thank you. We will manage," said Galax. "Well, if you'll excuse me, I have something else I have to attend to." He rose from the table and left the canvas.

Outside, the night air whisked wildly about. The rain clouds were still gathered heavily above, and although the showering rain had stopped, he felt a slight drizzle on his backside. Galax quickly made his way into the thick forest of Maia, and found a concealed place, where he could use the dagger.

He placed it in front of him, lit an orb of light, and read the inscription, *"Extendium, portcullis, cosmos."* It meant to open the *Gate of Worlds*. With a swift stroke, he sliced the dense air, and watched as the blade tore a thin segment of reality, in which he immediately walked through.

"Master...Master! Where *are you?"* he called. There was nothingness, quietness—an empty void. A light came from the distance that seemed artificial. Fragments of buildings flew past him, and linked up, like puzzle pieces, fitting themselves together where they belonged. He began to recognize where he was—in the city of Talfryn.

The streets where the festivity was to have taken place were empty. There were no crowds of celebrating townsfolk, birds, or any living thing for that matter. He did notice small portions of the scenery seemed to vanish when he passed. As he advanced on, he thought it strange to see the building walls began to fade, or as he guessed, become transparent. Now he could spot Elazar, sitting at a table in the library room of the wizard's temple. He was reading a book.

Elazar raised his eyebrows inquisitively, as Galax greeted him cheerfully. He had teleported himself inside the room, and was standing before him.

"Master, I am so happy to see you," he declared,

hugging him warmly.

"Galax, my dear lad, you're doing so well. I am strengthened by your efforts. I wish I could have been of more help to you, but every time I thought I was releasing myself from this prison, I found myself right back where I started. I've kept busy searching for answers in these ancient texts. However, I haven't been able to come across anything yet, to get me out of this spell-binder."

"I know, Master...I was told by Illustra that I could use the *Blade of Ismene* to contact you, but it is not useful in breaking the curse that is put upon you."

"Very well, I am to continue my research then," Elazar replied. "I know you have a key, Galax, but I forbid you to use it on me, at least not yet."

"Why Elazar, if it will get you out of here...why can't I?"

"Well, because there are more important matters than me. I don't want you to waste it. I have seen what you are doing, and it is of grave importance that you get to the next location, and use the key immediately. Amumet is dying, so you must hurry."

"Why can't I just give you the key, and you can use it now?" Galax suggested.

"It won't work here, Galax. You are still separated from me. The *Keys of Fate* won't activate in this forsaken zone. You should get to the next location, retrieve the key, and use it to change the *fate of the world*. Then you can free me from my confinement. Once I am liberated, you must get the other key to me. Do you understand?"

"Yes, Master. I will send you the key, as soon as I can."

"You have no choice but to continue your journey, Galax. Do not rest, until all the keys have been retrieved. There is still a chance Madicon will discover where one is hidden. Let me deal with him, when I have the opportunity to confront him again."

"Yes, Master," Galax echoed, flustered. He did not want to leave Elazar in this state.

"I will be fine. There is a lot of useful information here. I am catching up on old enchantments. They may come in handy later. You will do well to know what you will change, and keep it in your consciousness for the activation of the key. That's all I can tell you. If you need me, you know where to find me."

"Thank you, Master, for your advisement," Galax replied. "I will work as fast as I can."

"Go now, apprentice. I'll be waiting on you," Elazar insisted, turning the pages of an enormous book.

Nodding in reverence, Galax turned and plodded back the way he came. His mind was spinning with the weight of all that was said. He had a lot to think about, as far as what he wanted to change in the world, and he knew he had little time to do it.

He reached the rip in the veil of reality, and slipped right through it, finding himself back in the forest of Maia, once more. "*It is unusually dark tonight,*" he said aloud. He momentarily searched the face of twilight, admiring the vibrant stars that sparkled like fire-flies in the distance.

At this time, he missed his mother, the woman he could not really remember, except for her radiant aura and warm embraces. Trying not to feel sorry for himself, he headed back to the camp and found Fortress, who was waiting to hear the details of his little excursion.

"What did Elazar say?" Fortress asked when he had entered her tent.

"He has given me specific instructions. I am to use the next key to release him, and have the other one returned to him. He is counting on me. He says that Amunet is dying," Galax explained.

"I'm afraid it's much worse than we thought," Fortress added. "I have spoken to the *Silent Wispers*, and they have told me the moon is still on collision with Amunet. If we are to save our planet, we had better hurry."

"We still have a long ways to go yet, but we should reach the Genesis Sea in about a day and a half," Galax noted. "When we get there, I'll send Justise and Torin back with the key, while you and I continue on our quest."

"That's a good idea. Justise will be glad to return it to him for you."

"I wish there was a way we could get more news on what Madicon is up to."

"Maybe tomorrow, we can see what talents lay beneath Justise's skin. Perhaps she can give us a vision," she replied.

"Excellent, I never thought of that," raved Galax. "We will ask her, first thing tomorrow then."

"Good night, my dear friend," she muttered softly, as Galax yawned wearily.

"Night," he replied. In a matter of minutes, he had drifted off to sleep.

Chapter Fourteen
The Exodus

THE next evening, Justise was asked to delve deep into her visions to bring out details of the Ember Trolls, and what they were up to. She agreed, and with strained concentration, she was able to come up with a clear image of what could be expected in the next few days and weeks.

Far beneath the caverns of Mt. Nova, an enormous Ember Troll with veins of fire guarded the entrance to the chamber where a secret energy was hidden. He was only one of many Trolls that constantly labored over the construction of a powerful device, built for the primary purpose of rearranging the terrain, so that their kind could once again, live on the surface.

The plans for the engine came from the ancient vaults of the pyramid that was buried in the nexus of the great mountain. These designs were not of their world, but from an ancient race of sentient beings that were only legendary. They were thought to be long extinct from Amunet.

Only a few wizards knew of their existence, and among this league, there was plenty of debate on whether the strange beings had direct access to a pure source of ethereal energy. This energy was called *NeoShine*, and was known as the core element of *Light Making*.

The machine that used the *NeoShine*, was not of itself destructive, but with the tweaking of Madicon's enchantments, it was reconditioned for the intention of mass ecological devastation.

Madicon was making sure that the battle on Mt. Nova was going according to his king's wishes. Ismet Hasad was, thus far, in awe of his talents, and the switching of the bloodshed in his favor.

Kegan Wyntir kept his uncle's army focused, but from the mass amount of bodies that were lying slain on the battlefield, he was certain that they would not endure much longer. Nolan and his men could not get there soon enough. Justise thought of relaying this message to Nolan. She felt apt to persuading him to speed up his journey, before it was too late.

The Ember Troll known as Cros, focused the

NeoShine laser towards the northeast. His mouth seared with heat. Ash flickered and dropped from his arms, burning the dry, cracking ground around his thick feet. He stepped heavily in the correct position, and steered the navigational system 180 degrees into an exact position.

Unlike their cousins, the Woodland, Boonie, and Rock Trolls, the Ember Trolls could not survive the fresh air and harmonious atmosphere of Amunet. But neither could the Sea and Frost Trolls, who also resided close to the planet's heart. The Woodland and Boonie Trolls were the most defiant against their cousins, as they would be the least likely to exist for long, after the planet had changed from its natural form.

Justise witnessed the aftermath of the machine. It caused a great tsunami that flooded the swamps, forests and hills of the Genesis region. After hearing this, Galax thought it strange that all the keys seemed to be linked to the locations pointed at by the *NeoShine* beams. He pondered how this had happened, and if there was somehow a divine intervention, leading him towards a path he was unaware of.

"I'll never understand those creatures," Justise muttered in frustration.

"Why should you, you're not a Troll," said Galax.

"You need not to be a Troll, in order to understand one," said Fortress, disdainfully. "They're simply tired of their restriction, and merely searching for change."

"It makes no sense!" shrieked Justise.

"Then you should ask them," said Galax. "We must see exactly where their loyalty lies."

Fortress sighed. The very thought of it had occurred to her, but she had not yet come across a Troll, Woodland or otherwise, that would war against their kind.

"We shall see," she agreed.

By noon the whole army, including Galax and his followers, set out across the hills to the north. They rode through the forest of Maia, past the great lakes of Endico, and continued onward toward their destination. Prince Nolan was contented to be escorting and protecting Galax from an attack of Bloodwyns. He could not help but to wonder, though, what the Bloodwyns had to do with the saving of the planet, or why Galax was so eager to see his army winning the war.

Questions arose in his mind that he needed answering, and after a brief hesitation, he commanded his horse to gallop alongside Sugar Cane, who somehow always miraculously found his way back to Galax when he needed him.

"So tell me... I have heard whispers among my men, of a key of some sort?" he asked. "You spoke of ancient magic, and how it would give us the advantage."

Galax stared at him awkwardly. "Yes, there are many keys, and if any one of them falls into the hands of Madicon, all of Amunet will suffer.

Nolan became worried. He knew of the power of Madicon, and that Galax, although impressive, was really no match for him.

"Is there anything I can do to help?" he suggested.

"You have already been a tremendous help, especially back there, when we were being attacked by those Bloodwyns," said Galax. You could not have done more. Trust me."

"I'm glad we came when we did," Nolan replied, watching Torin sail above him. "If you need, I can spare a few of my men."

"No, *please*... That is very thoughtful of you, but my *magic* will suffice," Galax assured him. He was thinking that Nolan's men would only slow him down, or get in the way.

By nightfall, the entourage had arrived at a crossroad. They posted camp at the foot of a small hill. By morning, Nolan's army would continue heading towards the north, while Galax and his followers would turn sideways towards the east.

Galax checked the *Blade of Ismene*. It was apparent that it had not completely recharged. He shuddered, desiring to see Elazar again.

"You'll have to wait," said Fortress, noticing his irritation. "It shouldn't take much longer."

"Can't tell," said Galax. He handed her the blade to inspect.

"It has progressed halfway," she replied, handing it back.

"I'm headed into the cave, to look at the map," he declared. "Are you coming?"

Fortress considered. "Yes, I am very familiar with this region. I would like to see exactly where we are going. Perhaps I can find us a much faster route."

"Good, give me a few minutes, and I will let Justise know," he said.

It wasn't long before Galax and Fortress had gone deep into a pitch black tunnel, where the wind whistled through the abyss, sending chills up Galax's spine. He disliked dark places.

"What was that?" he uttered. An eerie piercing sound echoed behind them. Galax turned abruptly, catching a quick glimpse of a pair of white eyes that lit up the darkness. For a moment, he could not think. He had forgotten the chant for brightening up his light orb.

"Show yourself!" he demanded. Fortress was quiet. She knew what was lurking in the dark, so she stood a few paces behind Galax, waiting patiently for the scene to unfold.

The eyes moved slowly towards them, until it

finally reached the light gleam. Galax had nearly stumbled back in anticipation. He imagined something horrid, but it was only the wolf, Ulrike.

"Oh, it's just you," he said, holding his light orb closer to the wolf. "Why didn't you say something earlier, if you wanted to come?" he asked.

Ulrike looked up at him, buoyantly wagging his tail. "Well, come on then," said Galax, gesturing Ulrike onward. The wolf was all too eager to tag along. He had a mind to be a good watcher and protector for the apprentice.

They followed the path until Galax felt he was in an acceptable enough spot to activate the map. After the map was aglow, encompassing the whole area, Fortress pointed out the quickest route they would have to take in order to reach the Genesis Sea, before the whole region was destroyed by the fault line that had opened deep beneath the waves.

Little did they know that Ulrike understood exactly what was being said about the underwater quake. He was considering how this would affect his own wolf pack and their safety. But right now, they were far away, traveling at great speed towards the western shore.

"The widening of this crack worries me," Fortress stated. "I fear the worst is yet to come."

"Oh, but look at this, the key seems to be moving rapidly underneath the water. You see here?" He pointed to the holographic key, and followed it with his fingers. "I wonder why it is moving so fast."

"The question is not why it is moving, but what is moving it?" said Fortress. "I'm pretty sure it is attached to something monstrous—a large fish perhaps."

"I guess we'll have to wait and see," answered Galax. He was anxious, and ready to fix the planet's problem as soon as possible.

The air turned foggy, as Galax and his companions traveled east towards the Genesis Sea. The gray clouds were forming steadily above them, making thunderous noises, but no rain fell. Nolan and his men had gone towards the north, leaving early, even before the sun had begun to rise.

Nellie returned a few times, following them every few miles, before she disappeared over the horizon again. She had allowed the wind to carry her wings far, before resting every now and then on the nearby branches, or swooping down to perch serenely on Justise's arm. Torin flew swiftly in and out of the blustery sky, doing a free fall or two, just to arouse his adrenaline.

The Maia woods were becoming condensed with tall trees, bushes, and all manner of vegetation. They arrived at the edge of the woods, and stood before a babbling brook. Just beyond would be the valley of Labyrinthine, and further on they would run into the

Aether plains before they reached the Sea. There was still a long ways to go, but Galax was determined to make it by noon the next day.

As the darkness caressed a falling star, Fortress felt a strong presence in the shrubbery behind them. "Shhh," she said, looking around curiously.

"What is it?" whispered Justise.

"Listen—" she exclaimed, as everyone fell silent. "Do you hear that? I hear a heavy heartbeat."

"I can't hear anything," muttered Galax.

"You must keep moving, and I will catch up with you. There is something I have to do first."

"I'm not leaving you here," Galax protested.

"Come here, Galax," Fortress demanded. "Closer..."

Galax leaned closer to her.

"There is a Woodland Troll lurking nearby, and I plan to converse with it," she whispered softly.

"Are you sure?" Justise asked, startled, looking quickly behind her.

"Of course I'm sure. I know a Troll when I feel one. He won't speak to me unless I'm alone. So you'll all have to leave me for a while," she put in. "Don't worry, I won't take long."

"But it's *too dark*," Justise persuaded.

"I have my *Silent Wispers*. They will light the way," said Fortress.

"Alright, you go ahead then. We won't be too far,"

groaned Justise. She didn't trust any Trolls, not even the Woodland ones.

"Why not camp here for the night, and then we can leave first thing tomorrow?" Justise asked, after they had traveled down the path a bit.

"This is a nice spot," Galax agreed.

Deep in the brush of a hidden nook, Fortress listened to the *Silent Wispers*, as they circled around her transforming hair. She allowed herself to change, choosing a deep green color for her skin. The Woodland Troll stood quietly nearby, blending into the atmosphere, and waited for her to acknowledge him. She was small compared to his towering frame, and had to lean far back in order to look him squarely in the eyes.

"So, you've heard about your cousins?" asked Fortress.

The Troll stepped out from among the landscape, so he could be visibly seen. On his shoulders, arms, and feet, were patches of small trees, shrubbery, grass and undergrowth. He undoubtedly could have disappeared into the scenery, and nobody would have even noticed him. This was true of all Trolls, as they each had the ability to camouflage with nature, according to their genes.

"I have seen what my cousins mean to do," the Troll said. "Are you the Woodland fae they call Fortress?"

"Yes, and what is your name?"

"My name is Bae, and I speak for all of the Wood-land Trolls in this area. We would like to solicit your leadership. We are ready to serve you, *oh Elemental One.*"

"This is good, Bae!" said Fortress. "We do need

your help."

"What must we do?" asked Bae. "Our kinfolk in the swamps, the Boonie Trolls are being driven from their lands, and I have even heard the cries of my Sea cousins on the eastern shore."

"Follow the path to the north, and invade the Mountains of Nova. Galax, the apprentice will use his magic to help you, but you must do all you can to aid the armies of Osnath. If you can breach their territory, stop the Ember Trolls from using their machine."

"You can count on us, *Elemental One*," Bae thundered. "We will break through to our cousins, and cease their destruction."

"I wish I could go with you, but you know I must rescue the Sea. Good luck, my dear friend," said Fortress. "May the light guide your path."

As if on cue, the *Silent Wispers* flew gently upwards from their cubby holes in the nooks and crannies of Fortress' nature strands, and gathered around the tiny trees nesting on Bae, lighting up his face.

When Fortress returned to the camp, Galax was sitting alone by the fire, twiddling with the *Blade of Ismene*. "It has completely regenerated," he said.

"I see. Are you planning to use it again?" she asked.

"No...not yet. I will hold off, until I have a reasonable question to ask," Galax replied, putting the knife back in his garments. "What happened with the Troll?"

"There are many Trolls that wish to join us in the cause against their cousins," she said. "I have agreed to guide them, and have already given them a task."

"What task is it?"

"They will gather together to invade the Mountains of Nova, and try to destroy the eco-machine."

"That is good. Prince Nolan will need all the help he can get."

"Yes, I know. I hope they can get there soon. Trolls are very slow movers."

Galax chuckled optimistically. "At least they have tall legs to help them cover ground. Don't worry, Fortress, they're probably halfway there already."

"You're probably right, Galax."

"I saved you some dinner," he mentioned.

"I'm not hungry, but thanks anyway...so, where are Justise and Torin?" asked Fortress, after glancing between a set of pine trees. She did not see either of them.

"I believe they went for a walk near the lake," he replied nonchalantly. Fortress grinned hard at Galax.

"What?" he asked playfully, as he caught on to her witty behavior.

"Oh, nothing," she muttered. She couldn't help but wonder if Galax had ever been in love. It is none of my business, she thought, and rolled back on a rock to take a nap.

Justise and Torin were holding hands, strolling quietly by the silky lake. The beam of the pale moon swung down like a spotlight, and showered them with a slight brilliance. The *Silent Wispers* were glowing and fluttering about, making humming vibrations that sounded like a melody. At least Justise thought so. She was listening to it, when Torin turned abruptly to look at her, spreading his wings out so gently that she stood facing him with anticipation.

Torin set his feathery wings down around the both of them, and stared into Justise's anxious eyes. "I have grown very fond of you," he said. "You are all I have left to live for."

He touched her left cheek lightly with his hand, and then pulled back her hair. Justise was speechless. She nearly held her breath and leaned in for a kiss, in which Torin readily accepted.

They walked back to the campsite, and found Galax sleeping, while Fortress seemed to be talking to the *Silent Wispers* that circled her head. "What are they saying?" asked Justise, admiringly.

A wisp flew to Justise, and whispered in her ear. The glow of its lifeforce flickered vibrantly as it settled on her shoulder, flapping its wings. Justise smiled. She was in awe of the beauty and delicacy of such creatures, and curious of their mysterious ways.

"The *Silent Wispers* have been telling me of the movement of the Woodland Trolls, and their progress. They have readily agreed to align with us in hindering the use of the eco-machine. Now that they have stepped forward, it won't be long now, before the Boonie, and Rock Trolls are our allies, as well."

"That's good news," Justise said. "We can certainly use all the help we can get."

"This is wonderful," said Torin. He was normally the quiet one of the group, but this time, he insisted on giving his praise and comment. Indeed he was jubilant, and appreciative of the opportunity to help his friends in their quest.

They set out early the next morning, before dawn, traveling to the northeast. They had to follow the river for several hours, before reaching the plains, in which they stopped for a time to rest.

The wind blew a cool breeze that swayed the tall grass. Galax placed his hands above the grass, and smiled at the tickling of the tips on his palms. They were now ready to head into the Aether plains, which was only a few hours journey from the Genesis Sea.

Mounting their horses, each of them felt a heaviness fall on their hearts, as if they were becoming more and more connected with their surroundings.

"We're on the verge of discovering something," Justise remarked matter-of-factly. "I can feel it."

"I have felt it, too," said Fortress. "It is not a good

signal."

"Look at those dark clouds up ahead," said Torin, flying down to give his report. "A storm is coming."

"Well, we had better get moving then," said Galax. "We don't know how much time we have before this region is too dangerous for us to pass through."

Fortress nodded. "You are right, Galax."

Soon enough, Torin flew down again, anxious to give another report. This time, he had a great deal to reveal to them.

"I have seen many villagers, animals, and even a clan of Bog Trolls, heading in our direction," he said. "You'll see for yourself in a matter of minutes, as they are not that far from here."

Fortress glanced towards the horizon, using her incredible sense of sight. She noticed a large brownish figure moving in the distance. "I believe the *Boonies* are leaving their swamps, and the whole region is evacuating. It must be worst than we suspected. Boonie Trolls aren't easily driven from their homelands."

The wind sped up fiercely, as well as the horses, and before they knew it, they were passing up herds of deer, rabbits, squirrels, wild boar, and other small animals, all rushing away from the various parts of the Genesis region.

"What an annoying sound," yelled Justise, as many as fourteen baby boars, all squealing, drove past her horse.

The ground shook as several Bog Trolls, often called *"Boonie"* treaded by, doing their best to avoid injuring the smaller rodents that were vigorously running on their path. An extra thick, sludgy one paused suddenly, turned abruptly, and stared curiously at Fortress.

"You are the elemental one?" he asked, as a gunk of mud dripped from his chin and splattered to the ground. He had left a trail of mud in his tracks. His head and back were covered in moss, and on his arms were numerous slimy snails, clinging desperately to the slippery vines hanging from his chest.

"Yes, indeed I am," answered Fortress.

"Your plans we have agreed. We are joining forces to attack the mountains, as you instructed," he said.

"Thank you for your support," replied Fortress, "and good luck." The Boonie Troll nodded and continued on its way.

They came across a lengthy single file of many young women, all dressed magnificently in full flowing gowns of silk. On their heads, each wore a jeweled crown. The lead princess halted and bowed gracefully toward Galax when she saw him, then immediately turned towards her sisters to signal them to wait for a moment, until he and his companions had passed.

Galax was considered as good as royalty, for it was well known that any wizard held the highest respect of the land. He was recognized by his specially imported shoes. To them, only a wizard would wear such lavish style and patterning.

At the end of the line, a handsome prince sat comfortably on the spread hood of a giant cobra, playing the flute. The snake charmer's lovely sounds hypnotized the cobra, which swayed its body rhythmically side to side, feeling the music as it slid smoothly along the grass.

Farther into the plains, they passed another dynasty. This impressive king wore a stupendous blue feather, taken from the tail of a water phoenix—while he rode on a chariot pulled by two hefty blue lions. The emblem on the chariot was of immortality, and the lions sported manes that were littered with water crystals.

The colorfully draped women and children were acting seriously frightened. They spoke nervously in their native tongue, of the return of a powerful spirit that lived in the sea. Galax could understand their language quite well, and listened to a woman trying her best to soothe her child.

"Don't worry, little Lulu," she pleaded. "Papa will be alright. He is coming later." The small child nodded her head, wiped a tear from her eye, and hugged her mother intensely. The mother started singing a lovely, yet sad song. Around her, voices joined in, complimenting hers, and carrying the tune far out into the evening breeze.

Next, a strange sight caught Galax's attention. He watched in amusement as a miniature, but fully grown tree was being carried in the middle by two stocky wildebeests. The trunk of the tree hung in between, and was strapped to their backs by tied ropes and blocks of carved wood. A tiny tribe of humans, no taller than three inches, were standing on the stretched-out branches, yelling and shaking their fists erratically. They passed by quickly, and Galax noticed their painted faces, and the angry look they held in their eyes.

"Why are they so infuriated?" asked Justise.

"Isn't it obvious?" Galax replied. "They don't want to leave their homeland."

"I'm sure they feel defeated," said Fortress. "If they had an enemy they could actually fight against, they would do everything they could to protect their territory."

"Why do I get the feeling that an unpleasant surprise is waiting right around the corner?" Justise interjected, as she picked up unnatural vibrations flowing through the atmosphere.

"That is because we're almost there," said Fortress. "Today we save the sea, tomorrow we save the world."

Chapter Fifteen
Giants of the Sea

THEY headed out to the Genesis Sea, fully prepared for what they might witness. Fortress guided them towards the deep canyon that was actually the bottom of the ocean, now exposed to the harsh elements of wind and heat mixed together. As they rode up to the edge of the terraces of mud, the wind blew so fiercely, that neither of them could stay on their horses.

"Look at that! I can't believe it," exclaimed Justise, dismounting her restless horse. As soon as her feet hit the ground, the frightened animal took off for calmer territory, with Sugar Cane leading the way.

She stood just a few inches from the chasm, breathless and bewildered at the upheaval of the deep sea floor. Even from afar, they could see the abyssal plain had divided, revealing a narrow inter-space of oceanic ridges and mountainous chains. To the west of the fracture, the water receded slowly, while the east side flooded downward endlessly into the sunless void of timeless darkness. None of them wanted to slide down into the gloomy gulf of slime and dead plant and animal sediments, but each one sucked in their guts, and began their slushy march into the murky depths below. All of them did this, except Torin and Fortress, who both took to the sky, flying as fast as they could towards the center of the catastrophe.

Storm clouds gathered at the heart of the dev-astation, the spot where the landmass caved into never-ending trenches, taking in a tremendous downpour of continuous oceanic life. The gigantic waterfall stood over 200 meters, cascading with such force that schools of fish seemed to plunge from the heavens.

The air was growing heavy with mist, causing each of them to sweat wildly. Galax was speechless as he passed several large sea craters, sheltering various aquatic species that had somehow escaped to them from the toxic oxygen. The seabed flattened out a mile from the steep slopes of the terraces. They con-tinued down, passing flipping fish, flopping about in desperate attempts to find safe water holes and crevices.

Ulrike started growling ferociously when he caught sight of a gargantuan water form approaching him. He was startled by the towering mass, as it continually shifted, and so he ran towards it baring his sharp teeth. But it was only a Sea Troll, who sped forward, throwing himself on a huge Octopus, as it struggled to stay alive. He did this in order to protect it from the heat and the deadly gases in the atmosphere. Afterwards, two more Sea Trolls did the same, until they had created a watery barrier for which the octopus could move about freely.

Ulrike had a sudden sense of danger for his wolf pack. Since the beginning of the journey, he hadn't felt that way, but now he turned around and began to howl excessively. Torin had been flying as fast as he could towards the waterfall, but as soon as he heard Ulrike's outcry, he immediately stopped midair, and headed back to him.

"What's he doing?" asked Justise, glaring confusedly at Ulrike, as Torin landed in the mud.

"He's about to leave us." Torin answered. He could easily read Ulrike's mind. "Ulrike's instincts tell him to go back and warn his pack. He feels a threat to their lives."

"You mean that the Ember Trolls are targeting another area?" Justise asked dismally.

"Yes, and unfortunately, his pack is moving that

way."

Torin kneeled down, looking Ulrike in his eyes. They understood each other without having to speak words. He touched his cheek, and gave him a warm goodbye hug.

"Be safe, old boy," Torin said. "Go on...I can manage!" Ulrike whimpered and ran off towards the coastline. He stopped to turn around and glance back at Torin, and then ran off again.

Galax had stepped into a sink hole, and was just beginning to charm his way out, when he heard a loud noise that made everyone freeze in their tracks.

Looking up about 100 meters into the torrential falls, the shadow of a terrifying sea monster was seen swimming irritably to and fro. The air had turned incredibly tense all of a sudden, as Fortress hovered above the Troll made gap in the ocean floor.

"Here's the situation," Fortress telepathically said to Galax. "This isn't going to be easy. I will try and hold back the waterfall, while you cast an enchantment on it that can never be broken. Can you do that?"

"I'm not sure if I know any?" I might have to use the *Blade of Ismene*, and ask Elazar if he is aware of anything that will be unbreakable."

"Well, you better hurry then, because from the looks of this, there isn't much time," said Fortress. "I will do what I can, but this disaster may be too much for even me to handle."

Galax was afraid for Fortress. He could see that the ocean had a power and a force that could easily overtake her. He wished that she would wait, but he knew she would do everything she could to combat the floods, before he returned. He pulled out the blade and sliced the air, forcing the scenery to change at will. A moment later and he was back in the temple, staring quizzically at Elazar, as he was pouring over his books.

"Galax, what is happening?" asked Elazar. He was nervous, for he felt Amunet's grumbling. "Why have you come? Do you have the *key*?"

"No, I need an enchantment that will bond the belly of the Genesis Sea from pouring down into the planet's core, and taking every living sea-thing with it."

"I understand. This is serious. I have taught you many binding charms, but to seal a wall of power of this magnitude, you'll need the strongest tie. Perhaps the *Seal of Eternity* will do the trick."

"Here, let me find it for you." Elazar took several moments to sort through a stack of large editions, until he found the heavy book he was looking for. His hands shivered slightly as he pealed back its antique pages, and flipped to a one where the spell was written.

"Thank you," said Galax, as he touched the

page, committing to memory the entire text. With the stroke of his hand, he had the gift to remember graphically, every detail that had been written.

When he returned, Fortress was nowhere to be seen. All of a sudden, Torin appeared, flying out of nowhere, frenzied and wet.

"What happened?" Galax yelled.

"Fortress has gone inside the waterfall, and she is searching for the key. She says she believes it is on the shell of a giant Sea Turtle, a crystal-back."

Just then, Fortress appeared transformed into the element of water, standing before them like shimmering light. She waved Galax towards her, and urged him to start the enchantment. Galax stood below the sheet of sheer liquid expanse, gazing upwards, pulling within him all the emotional energy he had in his soul. He stretched out his hands, and called out the text, creating a barrier that stopped the flowing of the sea from delivering up its pool of contents.

There was a lightning rod that beamed across it, and like an unseen drape, it welded into an eternal shield.

Behind them, Justise stood by a sunken ship. It piqued her curiosity, and she decided to have a look inside. The ship was wrecked, wooden, and old. It held many mysterious secrets, and for some odd reason, she felt a strange connection to it.

Once inside the hull, she felt the pull of a vision coming on. She saw the captain, and the men who had plunged their bodies into the sea, as the ship, burning from within, slowly sank to the floor. But it was the face of one of the drifters that struck a chord in her nerves. For it wasn't just any man, but the lover of Muriel, Rimi McCracken, the ghost that had kidnapped her. She didn't linger long inside the dilapidated cargo hold, and after several moments of staring at his fading mirage, she turned away and ran out of the ship, scanning the scenery for any sign of Torin.

When she caught a glimpse of him, she yelled, "Where's Galax?"

"You just missed him," he replied, stretching his white wings out as far as they could yield. "He went into the waterfall, in search of the key."

Deep beneath the sea, Galax swam quickly towards the giant crystal-back sea turtle and her babies. The mother turtle's gemstone shell was incredibly sharp and spiky. The key was embedded in one of the crystals, so Galax had to think fast as to how he was going to distract the giant sea creature.

His plan was simple. He would lure the turtle by projecting a body double, and then creep aboard its back, while his other self was being attacked. *I'm not sure if this will work, but it's worth a try,* he thought.

Galax had one important thing to fear. Crystal-back sea turtles possessed a special energy source they stored in the crystals on their shells. This defense mechanism was laser sharp, and as hot as molten lava.

He positioned himself in front of the turtle, and began to swim towards her. He could see the tension in her eyes, as she began charging up her crystal spikes. All the sparklers lit up, and after a moment, his body double was evading hot, laser-beam mouth blasts that melted everything in its path. While his second self was busy using shielding spells, and dodging back and forth, nearly as fast as the speed of light, Galax swam his way in from the rear, and climbed aboard the turtle's back.

He grabbed a firm grip on a tall spike, and

scanned the whole carapace for the one with the key. After a few minutes, he spotted it embedded near the hub. With all his force, he pulled and jiggled it as hard as he could, but the sparkler wouldn't budge. Suddenly, the turtle began swimming rapidly upward. He had no choice but to brace himself by holding on to the spikes. *"Displacious Crystium,"* he managed to utter, commanding the crystal to shake loose from the shell. Amongst numerous bubbles, it floated evenly into his hand. His body double was no longer of interest to the turtle, and she was now setting her course on a different path.

The crystal-back turtle broke the surface of the water, bursting from the shadows of murkiness, and into the chill of what was now calm weather. Although the wind was still raging violently, the rain had completely stopped, and the lightning boomed farther in the distance.

Galax was contented now. He finally had two keys in his possession, and he knew exactly what needed to be done to make things right again. He glanced back, and observed the baby turtles swimming behind their mother, along with the currents. The little fire-breathers didn't even notice that he was there, as they bobbed, dipped, and plunged their bodies in and out of the water. By now, there was quite a bit of steamy bubbles rising from beneath him.

To the east, Fortress had gone into the eye of the

storm. She had managed to calm the weather down a great deal, but there was still the issue of the numerous chunks of debris that was hurling through the sky. She found herself trying desperately to decrease the amount of energy that the storm was picking up.

Torin flew down near the turtle, yet keeping a measurable distance away, so as not to provoke her. Galax squinted at Torin, and waved his arms. "You need to take this key back to the castle and deliver it to Elazar," he ordered. "You and Justise will have to go on without me. Fortress and I will continue our quest, and we will all meet up at a later date."

"Don't worry, Galax. We'll get it to him," Torin hollered, flapping his wings rigorously. Galax cast a charm on the key, and watched it fly up into the air and into Torin's palm.

"Be safe, my dear friend," Galax cried, surveying his supporter, as he flew beyond the horizon.

Chapter Sixteen
The Turning of the Tides

MADICON sat hunched over in a narrow wooden chair. Two Bloodwyns flew restlessly about, ranting incoherently to themselves. For a second, Madicon just stared at them cold-heartedly, and then unexpectedly lashed out in anger.

Red-eyed and irritated, he shrieked, "How dare you come back empty-handed! You might as well have not shown your face around here. If you know what's good for you, you'll get back out there, and finish what you've started."

The Bloodwyns were so spooked by his hostility towards them that they immediately flew up and away, without saying so much as a word of rebuttal.

At the heart of the Genesis Sea, Galax stood up

on the turtle's back, and reached into his wet satchel. He pulled out the key and the cube, and stood there meditatively—as the waves rocked his turtle float unsteadily this way and that. He had been thinking about this moment for the whole of the journey. Now it was time to put his thoughts into action, and clean up the mess that his enemies had made.

The list he'd memorized was detailed and extensive. The promise he'd made to Prince Nolan weighed heavily on his mind. He turned towards the storm clouds, sensing Fortress was near.

"It won't be long now, Fortress," he said aloud.

Putting the key to his lips, he kissed it gently, and placed it in the antique keyhole. Focusing his mind on the task, he began to slowly turn the key, mentally rearranging the world.

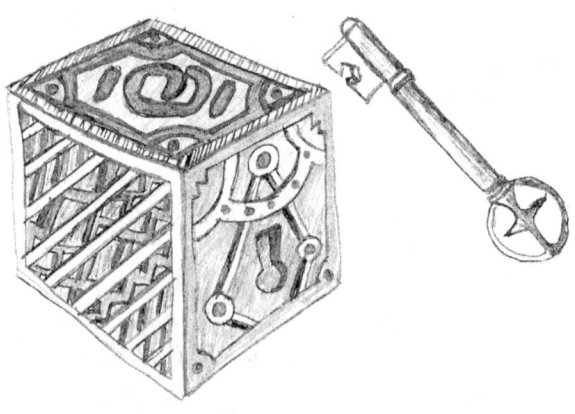

As he reflected on these corrections, the cube receded into itself, and all that was left was a small bright orb. The orb grew brighter and brighter, until he was blinded by its electrifying light. He felt himself vaporizing, as if he was fading into one dimension, and into another.

He could clearly see changes being made around him. It was his thoughts taking shape, shifting the destiny of Amunet. Elazar was the first to be restored to his rightful place, removed from the curse, and put safely back in the castle fort, without the Bloodwyns or Madicon in sight. The army of Osnath was now winning the war against King Hasad—the tall, redwood trees of the Shikoba forest were gradually growing their leaves back—and most of the atmospheric destruction of the world was being renewed to balance.

There was a great burst of energy, and then he saw something fall out of the sky and hit the water with an immense splash. It floated there for less than a second, before he recognized the elemental fae.

Before he could do anything to help, two strange aquatic creatures appeared out of nowhere. One of them swam up to her body, grabbed her and plunged underwater, carrying her with him.

"HEY, WAIT!" Galax yelled. "STOP...where are you taking her?" But the other creature just stared at him in an odd sort of way, and then quickly dived below.

From what Galax could tell, their heads resembled fish. They had fins, scales, and gills, but with elongated bodies that were human in form. Before he could think straight, he jumped into the water, and swam after them.

Following the sea creatures wasn't easy, and although he used magic to breathe underwater, he began getting dizzy as he swam for what seemed like eternity. Before he passed out, he caught a glimpse of a great mass of shimmering light, gazing in awe as the two beings disappeared into it.

Galax awakened lying on a long, white table. The room was bare and exceptionally bright. His head was laden with pain. As he sat up, he felt nauseous. Putting his hand to his forehead, he glanced around in suspicion. The room opened up a rectangle hole, and Fortress appeared. She was attentive, and quite eager to speak to him.

"What just happened? Who are these creatures? Where are we?" he anxiously questioned.

"Relax, Galax, lay back and *relax*...I'll tell you everything I know...I *promise*. But first you have to get some rest."

"Are we *safe* here?" he asked.

"Yes, my dear friend...we are. It is quite fascinating," she answered.

Galax lay back down on the table, and stared up

at the vibrant ceiling. He could tell that the walls were breathing the breath of life. For some odd reason, he felt at peace, and soon he was dreaming of his childhood, drifting softly into a subconscious state.

Many miles away, Justise and Torin were racing towards the southwest, headed for the castle mount. Elazar, now released from his prison, attempted to contact Galax, but couldn't get through to him. This didn't exactly worry him, but he was anxious to hear a full report of what had transpired during the turning of the key.

The millennial ritual still had to take place, and as soon as he could get the information he needed, he would perform it immediately. He knew that the key would be on its way, and so he walked into the room of orbs, triggering their activation, and settled down for a seeing session.

His favorite orb was made of azeztulite, a milky white rock with flecks of gold embedded in the stone. Elazar caressed the surface of the stone, invoking an instant connection. The azeztulite was called Naima, meaning "tranquility". Naima showed him the Ember Trolls, and how frustrated they were at the amount of restoration that clearly set them back a great deal.

All in all, Elazar was becoming comforted by the things he was witnessing. The world of Amunet seemed soothed, however something still wasn't quite right. The orb made of pearl, called Aysel, meaning "moonlight", called to him for attention.

His fingertips skimmed the orb, and began to faintly tremble at its cold touch. His eyes became cloudy and glazed. He saw the moon of Duldron, and how close it was moving to Amunet. He wondered if Galax had forgotten to change the fate of the moon. *What went wrong, or was this some kind of premonition?*

Aysel changed his vision abruptly, in response to his new line of questioning. Deep in the heart of Mt. Nova, the Ember Trolls were hard at work. Cros sat at the enormous eradicative machine, and pointed it towards the moon. He lifted a heavy green gemstone from a compartment, and placed it in a slot on the control bar. The gemstone was a gaia stone, made from the ash of Mt. Nova. This stone had special healing properties and was connected with the heart of Amunet. Elazar wondered how their using the stone was going to effect the destruction of their next target.

This time, they clearly aimed to scatter the remnants of Duldron all across the planet in order to do the greatest amount of damage, in the shortest amount of time. *It will surely be the beginning of the end,* he thought.

"Where is that key?" he said aloud. "This doesn't look good."

Aysel quickly showed him where Justise was located, riding her horse as fast as she could. She had
gained much ground, traveling non-stop towards the
castle. He knew it would take her more than a couple
of days to reach him. Torin was moving even faster
than she was, flying over trees and keeping a good
watch over her.

Elazar was just about to teleport to Justise when
all of a sudden he caught a glimpse of Galax. He was
resting in a special place. It was nothing like anything he had ever seen, but he had heard of it. It was
a place beyond the boundaries of Amunet—a place
of legend. He knew he had to try and connect with
Galax again. He concentrated on projecting his image towards him, and this time, he was successful.

Galax woke up blurry-eyed and displaced. He
lifted his head slightly off the table, thinking he was
seeing Elazar standing in front of him.

"Galax, hear my voice, and listen," Elazar said in
a commanding tone.

"Yes, Master...I'm listening," Galax replied, real-
izing what was happening. He was fully awake now,
and focused on keeping the link with Elazar strong
for as long as he could.

"You are very blessed to be where you are. These
beings mean you no harm. They are ancient and hold
a very special place in the universe. You must treat
them with every respect, and listen to whatever they

tell you, because if they have made contact with you, it is for a very good reason."

"Yes, Master...I understand," Galax replied.

"You have done well with the key. I am certain. However, your passage is not yet complete. You must retrieve all of the keys. To recover the last key, you have to unlock the mystery of your life, and set yourself free. I cannot rest until each and every key is returned safely to the castle."

"You can count on me, Master."

"Your friends are true, so do not forsake them. They will help you reach your destiny."

"Master, I've noticed that the keys have made their way into the oddest locations. I found both keys at the center of disaster, made by the Ember Trolls. Why is this happening?"

"The keys have positioned themselves where they thought it required. They didn't want you wasting valuable time searching for them, when Amunet needed your rescue the most."

"Are you saying that the keys are alive?"

"Yes, in the same way that the precious stone orbs have life, the keys are connected to your life force. The energy that you give them will be sent back to you to help you on the journey of awakening your spirit. Your life will become more meaningful, and thus you will be able to reach the full potential of why you are here."

"So, I guess I'm on a double quest, then? I should be more mindful of this."

"You have already come very far, my apprentice. Continue on your mission, and stay focused on the goal at hand," chimed Elazar. "I will always be with you."

With that being said, he faded away, and Galax sat there contemplating what he had been told.

After he snapped back into the awareness of his surroundings, Elazar realized what he had to do next. He didn't want to waste a single moment longer. He readied himself for his teleportation to Justise and Torin in order to catch them before Madicon or the Bloodwyns intercepted them and took the remaining key.

Elazar began his teleportation, thinking of Justise, and within a flash of light, he was standing somewhere.... However, it was not where he had intended to be. As he lingered at the edge of a great cliff, he witnessed the sight of a lifetime.

Moon-dust fell softly from a darkened, unsaturated sky, like snowflakes in the sand. The ground was completely covered with its speckles. There were colossal nuggets of moon fragments floating in the skies. Huge hunks of moon-crust were also rooted in the ground. Amunet was sick with grief. The floor beneath was unyielding, totally unable to sustain the lives of most of the species that lived on her surface.

Elazar kneeled down and touched the soil. His white robe became dingy with flakes. He was heart-broken, furious, and confused. He didn't know why he hadn't reached Justise, or where he was in time. All he knew was that something had gone terribly wrong during his departure.

Picking up a handful of moon-dust, he screamed a fierce and piercing yell that echoed out into the vast canyon. There were no birds that flew away, nothing but the silence of a dying planet, the one he loved and vowed to protect.

Chapter Seventeen
An Unimaginable Tale

FORTRESS came back into the room, and grinned at Galax. She was excited because she believed she was one of the first to have contact with the sentient beings of legend. She had heard many stories about them, and each one told tales of the Genesis Sea. She was guessing that she was going to find out answers to some of the mysteries her kind had been questioning for lifetimes. She could hardly contain herself.

"What's so amusing?" Galax asked, noticing how positive Fortress had become.

"In a minute you're going to witness something, and it's going to change your life forever," Fortress said, watching him stand to his feet.

"Well...what is it then?" he pestered. "And what is going on with this place? Elazar told me we were beyond Amunet."

"You talked to Elazar?"

"Yes, he projected himself here a few minutes ago. He said we were being given a rare chance," Galax answered, as he wandered about the empty room.

"He was right," she said boldly. "Now that you're awake, I have a feeling we're about to find out just how great our advantage is."

Galax was confused, but he listened to her anyway.

"Shhh....don't say anything," she gestured. "Be quiet for a minute."

Fortress didn't move or even breathe. She just stood there in silence staring at the shimmers of light around her. For a brief period, time seemed to stand still, and then the walls began dividing apart and shifting into several oblong segments. Eventually they morphed into human-like figures, but still remained a vision of swirling light particles.

The next thing he knew he was completely surrounded by seven light beings, and in the space between was a visage of stars. They spoke without moving their mouths, or he could hear their thoughts, he wasn't sure which one. He listened:

700,000 years ago, we came to this planet in search of a new life. Our kind have transcended this world, and moved on to the next dimension, but we still watch over the inhabitants here. We are your ancestors, and we want you to survive the fate that Amunet is about to endure. It has happened before, and will happen again, as all things in the universe repeat over time. When once we encountered the same fortune as you, we all had to transcend to remain in tranquility. We want to share with you the means to that destiny.

We created the Keys of Fate, and locked away a part of our being. Each and every cube is made up of NeoShine, the core element of Light Making. Take this neo particle, and ingest it—and we all will be with you.

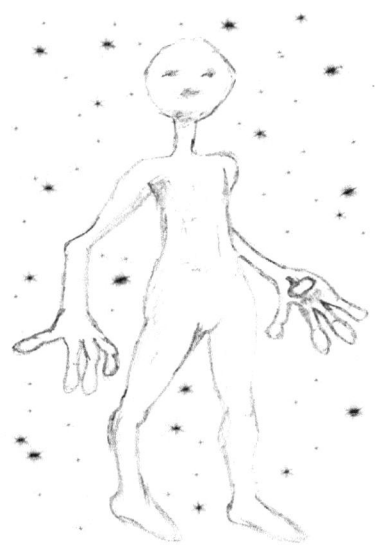

Galax kept quiet, while a particle was placed in the palm of his hand by one of the beings. He gazed at its profoundness, before putting it in his mouth and swallowing.

"The key to fulfillment is now inside of you. Use it wisely, and share it with the rest of the world," they said.

"Wait!" Galax objected, as he saw them fading into obscurity. "What do you mean? I don't understand!" Within a second of their disappearance, Galax found himself waking up on the shores of the Genesis Sea, with Fortress passed out next to him.

"Wake up?" he said, shaking her. "Wake up...are you all right?"

"Yes, I'm fine, Galax," she replied, although she felt as if she had been sleeping for a hundred years.

"What just happened?" he asked.

"The beings told us what we had to do in order to save ourselves from the same fate that they had," she said, shaking the sand out of her hair.

"What...what beings?" he said. "What are you talking about? I saw you fall out of the sky, and nearly drown. You must have gotten thrown from the storm. It's all my fault, by the way. I should have warned you when I was ready to use the key."

"You mean, you don't remember anything?" Fortress asked unhappily. "You can't have forgotten the whole *NeoShine* particle incident? It just happened a moment ago. It was incredible."

"Sorry, Fortress...I think you must have really bumped your head a little too hard when you hit the water. Why don't you just lay your head down for a little while, and I'll go and catch us some fish. I'm starving," Galax replied, jumping to his feet and rubbing his palms. "What type of fish do you think I might be able to catch out here? I've got my heart set on one of those jumbo Dragontooth. They're the tastiest."

"Oh, well...alright then. Since you can't seem to remember anything, I'll get the fire started so we can eat right away."

While Galax was fishing, she gathered sticks and stones, and made a pit. A quick touch of her finger to the firewood caused a pretty extensive discharge of flames. She sat on a huge rock, facing the sea, and watched Galax using a little magic of his own. With the enchantment of magnetism, he lured the fish right out of the water, and into his arms.

"Great *catch!*" she exclaimed.

Galax waved back at her, and gave her a cheerful salute. Although he was quite engaged in catching his prey, he wondered how far Justise and Torin had gone, hoping they were safely crossing the plains without encountering any Bloodwyns. *I'll have to contact Elazar as soon as I get this fish in my belly,* he thought. He heard his stomach growling.

"Wow, that's a big one, Galax," Fortress admitted, as Galax brought over his catch. "This is a feast for your eyes and stomach."

"Yes—too bad Justise and Torin aren't here. I know for a fact that Justise would have been impressed with this treat. You know how she is—she has a taste for rare delicacies."

"Yes, and Torin would have loved fishing with you. Shikoba are great fishermen, you know."

"Are they...well then, we could have made it a competition," Galax remarked.

"Come to think of it, I'm sure Ulrike would have beaten the both of you," Fortress chuckled, turning the fish over in the fire.

The sun was setting low in the east, and Galax felt a cool breeze blowing in the trees. They were camped near a small forest, and he was sure they weren't far from one of many deserted villages.

After he had eaten, Galax attempted to project to Elazar, as he found it strange that he had not yet heard from him.

"What's wrong?" Fortress asked, noticing Galax's perturbed face.

"It's Elazar. I haven't been able to make any connection with him. It's odd. I know I released him from Madicon's enchantment. This just isn't like him."

"Keep trying then and I'll send for the *Silent Wispers* to deliver a message to my sister, and see if she has heard any news of his captivity. I'm sure we'll be able to hear something in a little while."

Galax felt unsettled. His instincts told him something wasn't right. "You do that, please, and I'll check the holographic map. Something tells me the Ember Trolls have already chosen their next target. If my perception is correct, the next key will be in the center of it."

He pulled the pyramid from his satchel, and placed it on the rock in front of him. The atmosphere lit up easily with the grid, as he had mastered the technique of mentally activating it. The object that was supposed to represent the moon was now over-powering the hologram.

Suddenly, Fortress felt a sharp pain in her chest, as she watched the movement on the map. A large beam of green light was shooting straight for the moon. Her heart nearly stopped, as she realized what the Trolls had set as the next target.

"It's the moon, Galax!" Fortress exclaimed.

"That can't be right!" said Galax, in awe of their audacity. "The Trolls wouldn't go that far, would they?"

"Who knows how far they are willing to go," said Fortress. "Come to think of it, I sent for the *Silent Wispers*, and they should have been here by now. We'd better get to the next key, before those Trolls cause a major catastrophe to the whole of our solar system."

"But how do we get there? The next key is moon bound," asked Galax, zooming in on the map.

"I have no idea," said Fortress, helping Galax put out the last flame of the fire. "But we'll think of something."

"You're probably right. We won't know, unless we try," said Galax reassuringly.

Fortress gathered her thoughts, forcing her mind to remain open to the possibilities, and pointed to the illuminated skyline. Galax gave an earnest smile, relieved that there was still an ounce of hope, as the moon slowly descended towards them.

To Be Continued....